Roderick turned and nearly bowled over the petite young woman who had sprung from nowhere to stand directly in his path

"Darling! Thank you. Are we ready to leave now?"

In a single motion almost faster than the eye could follow, she lifted the sable coat from his careless fingers. He had only an instant to notice the shocking bit of glittery green that posed as a dress on her provocative form before both were concealed in the folds of the coat.

"What the devil do you think you're doing?"

She didn't even look at him. Her gaze searched the crowd. Instinctively he raised his head to see what had caused the flash of fear that darkened her lively blue eyes. He was still surveying the crowd when, without warning, she stretched up on her toes. Clasping his face, she tugged it down to within inches of her own. Her lips covered his.

"Please help me," she whispered.

SECRET CINDERELLA
DANI SINCLAIR

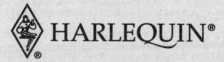

HARLEQUIN®

TORONTO • NEW YORK • LONDON
AMSTERDAM • PARIS • SYDNEY • HAMBURG
STOCKHOLM • ATHENS • TOKYO • MILAN • MADRID
PRAGUE • WARSAW • BUDAPEST • AUCKLAND

For Scott, Megan and Amanda; Ciara, Lisa and Rachel;
Justin and Rick; Evan, Trevor, Kyle and Ryan;
Mike, Eddie, Rene and Michele, because family
is important. And for Roger, Chip, Dan and Barb,
as ever. Love you guys!

ISBN 0-373-22827-9

SECRET CINDERELLA

Copyright © 2005 Patricia A. Gagne

All rights reserved. Except for use in any review, the reproduction or utilization of this work in whole or in part in any form by any electronic, mechanical or other means, now known or hereafter invented, including xerography, photocopying and recording, or in any information storage or retrieval system, is forbidden without the written permission of the publisher, Harlequin Enterprises Limited, 225 Duncan Mill Road, Don Mills, Ontario, Canada M3B 3K9.

All characters in this book have no existence outside the imagination of the author and have no relation whatsoever to anyone bearing the same name or names. They are not even distantly inspired by any individual known or unknown to the author, and all incidents are pure invention.

This edition published by arrangement with Harlequin Books S.A.

® and TM are trademarks of the publisher. Trademarks indicated with ® are registered in the United States Patent and Trademark Office, the Canadian Trade Marks Office and in other countries.

www.eHarlequin.com

Printed in U.S.A.

ABOUT THE AUTHOR

An avid reader, Dani Sinclair didn't discover romance
novels until her mother lent her one when she'd come
for a visit. Dani's been hooked on the genre ever since.
But she didn't take up writing seriously until her two
sons were grown. With the premiere of *Mystery Baby*
for Harlequin Intrigue in 1996, Dani's kept her computer busy ever since. Her third novel, *Better Watch Out,*
was a RITA® Award finalist in 1998. Dani lives outside
Washington, D.C., a place she's found to be a great
source for both intrigue and humor!

Books by Dani Sinclair

CAST OF CHARACTERS

Melanie (Mel) Andrews—The white sheep amongst a family of thieves, she thought she'd escaped her criminal legacy. Now she must use her unusual skills to find a killer.

Roderick Laughlin III—— The wealthy CEO plays Prince Charming for a night—and finds he's helped a beautiful woman flee a murder scene.

Gary Andrews—Mel's brother may be a genius when it comes to writing computer programs, but he's already wanted for burglary. Could he have added murder to the charges?

Carl Boswell—Roderick's vice president didn't intend to die. But did he intend to sell out Roderick, or was he trying to trap a thief?

Claire Bradshaw—Mel's neighbor and good friend has moved on from her own shady past. Or has she?

Harold DiAngelis—Gary's co-worker moonlights as a security guard. Has he moved into the big leagues with murder and theft?

Shereen Oro—The international model has been dating Roderick exclusively for the past several months, but she isn't above flirting with the competition.

Larry Wilhelm—The CEO of Roderick's chief competition may want to compete for more than just business.

Prologue

"Mel?"

Melanie Andrews gripped the phone more tightly and hit the mute button on the television remote.

"Gary? What's wrong?"

Her brother's sigh carried clearly to her ear.

"I'm in a jam. I need a favor."

Seven years older, her brother had never once asked for anything resembling a favor.

"Name it."

She sensed his wry smile, but it was the ragged sound of his breathing that sent her heart skidding nervously in her chest.

"How rusty are your skills?"

Her mouth went dry. She'd known the moment she heard his voice he was in trouble, but this…

"How sharp do they need to be?" she asked nervously.

"There's a New Year's Eve party tonight in the hospitality suite at the Rorhem Hotel downtown."

Her stomach contracted. He pushed out words as if the effort were painful.

"Carl Boswell is going to pass a DVD to someone at that party. I need you to steal it first."

She inhaled sharply. "Boswell is the man from RAL who was going to buy your program."

"Yeah. He decided to steal it instead." The ironic tone he tried for was lost in the sound of his labored breathing.

"You're hurt."

He ignored the interruption. "Six-four, two-thirty. Sandy red hair. Sharp widow's peak."

He was fading fast. Her stomach twisted with fear. "I'll get the DVD. I'll bring it to you."

"No!"

The crack of the word sent all sorts of terrified images springing to mind.

"I won't be there," he said more calmly. "I have a place to go."

"What's wrong with you?"

"Don't worry about it."

Worry nothing. She was scared to death. "If you die on me, I'll never forgive you."

He managed a weak chuckle that ended on a cough. "Not a chance, kid."

He wasn't going to tell her. Her mind was busy supplying all sorts of horrible scenarios, but she tried to keep her voice steady by focusing on what he really needed.

"How will I know I have the right DVD? Is it labeled?"

"Might be now." He paused, his voice growing more ragged with each breath.

"Never mind. If he has more than one, you'll get a collection," she promised. Mel could almost hear his slow smile.

"Be careful. He likes knives."

"Gary!"

"Get the program back for me, kid, it's the only copy I made. Of course that bastard could have made more by now."

Her fingers pressed tightly against the plastic of the telephone.

"You didn't back it up?"

Gary had been working on this program for well over a year now. Not being a computer person, the only thing she knew about his pet project was that it was some sort of security system he was very excited about.

"I can re-create it, Mel, that's not the point."

"Okay. Never mind." He sounded so weak. "I'll retrieve your brainchild, but you'll owe me big," she added fiercely, trying not to let him know how scared she was for him.

"Be careful. Boswell's willing to kill for it. I don't want to be an only child, either."

Her heart plummeted to her toes, her wild imaginings reinforced. But she kept her tone light, trying not to let him hear her fear.

"Mom and Dad would be ticked," she agreed. "Don't worry, Gary, he'll never feel a thing."

Chapter One

Mel hated it when her words turned prophetic.

Carl Boswell had been past feeling anything at all when she found him. Now she clutched the slim plastic card and the keys she'd removed from his wallet an instant before she'd been discovered going through the dead man's pockets. She continued to ignore the horrified, sick feeling in her stomach as she paused to get her bearings. She didn't have time for sick. Not then, and especially not now.

From the elevated balcony, Mel frantically scanned the noisy crowd below, landing on a tall, imposing figure in an immaculately tailored tuxedo. The stranger moved alertly among the room's occupants, nodding to acquaintances, but not stopping to speak to anyone. His purposeful stride was carrying him toward the exit at the far end of the ballroom.

Perfect.

As she skimmed down the stairs keeping her gaze focused on the man, she watched him pinch the bridge of his nose as though he had a headache. Understandable in this din.

He continued on his path with the sense of purpose that had first drawn her eyes—a lean, feral cat among the pigeons. People parted instinctively to let him pass.

Not a good mark. He was too alert for that. But she was desperate and his size alone might present a shield. He'd have to do. Everyone else seemed to be with someone.

She shot a glance over her shoulder. Still clear.

Mel darted amid the clusters of people while trying to keep him in sight. Her spiked heels didn't add nearly enough height. Fortunately, the stranger was lofty enough that his perfectly groomed, thick dark hair stayed visible.

Another glance over her left shoulder confirmed the worst. Someone had figured out where she'd gone. A tall man in a perfectly fitted tuxedo appeared on the balcony near the entrance she'd just used.

He was not alone.

Mel bit back a groan of dismay. This was bad—very bad. With an imperious sweep of his arm, the man sent two burly security men scurrying into the crowd.

Looking for her.

Her throat went dry. Renewed adrenaline sent her pulse racing faster. Now she blessed her short stature as she ducked behind a man and woman who blocked the aisle. They chatted with a table full of laughing people, oblivious to the others around them. Mel managed what she hoped was a cheerful smile as she edged around the couple, aware of several startled looks from some of those seated there.

Cursing the shiny beacon of a glittery dress she wore, she kept moving. Her choices had been severely limited after Gary's frantic call, and the borrowed dress had accomplished its original purpose. No one had questioned her right to join the noisy private party upstairs when she timed her arrival to coincide with a large, boisterous group.

Up there, the gaudy dress had been an asset. Unfortunately, most of the women down here had opted for black, which meant that any minute now one of the men pursuing her would spot the bright kelly-green color. If she could make it to the tall stranger she had a slim chance of getting away.

RODERICK LAUGHLIN DRUMMED his fingers in annoyance as he waited for the coats. His headache seemed to be growing in direct proportion to the noise. The blue haze of cigarette smoke wafting in from the balcony outside added yet another layer to his discomfort. He'd had more than enough frivolity for one evening. As soon as his companion came off the dance floor they were leaving.

Parties like this were Shereen's forte, not his. To see and be seen was everything in a modeling career and Shereen relished every moment. Roderick, on the other hand, had never been fond of large crowds but he'd promised to bring her tonight, so he had. Still, enough was enough. In his opinion, there were better ways to start a new year.

The pain in his head lightened a bit as he pictured several alternatives. Unfortunately, Shereen wasn't likely to want to spend the early hours of the new year in bed when she could be dancing and drinking and posing to be admired. Convincing her to leave would probably cost him a fortune for some trinket that had caught her eye. Roderick didn't care. He wanted to go home.

The young woman manning the coatroom set aside some sort of textbook she'd been studying and returned promptly with his topcoat and the full-length sable fur that had been his Christmas present to Shereen. Shereen wasn't interested in being politically correct and the coat had caused more than one furrier to throw up his hands in despair. She'd insisted on an exact match for her shoulder-length dark sable tresses. Now that brunettes were all the rage on the runway, the silver fox fur that had matched her hair last year was no longer adequate.

Roderick rubbed fiercely at his temple as he withdrew his wallet and generously tipped the tired-looking woman behind the counter. Anyone who could study an anatomy text in this crush deserved all the help she could get. Her face brightened in gratitude when she saw the bill's denomination.

With her heartfelt thanks echoing in his ears, he shrugged into his coat and lifted Shereen's. Mentally he had to admit that the garment had been worth all the effort. Shereen looked exquisite framed in fur, particularly when the coat was all she wore. But then, Shereen looked terrific in anything—and especially in nothing at all. It was her most endearing quality.

Roderick turned, deep in rumination of his new plans for ushering in the new year, and nearly bowled over the petite young woman who had sprung from nowhere to stand directly in his path.

"Darling! Thank you. Are we ready to leave now?"

In a single motion almost faster than the eye could follow, she lifted the sable from his careless fingers and disappeared inside. He only had an instant to notice the shocking bit of glittery green that posed as a dress on her provocative form before both were totally concealed in the voluminous folds of the coat.

"What the devil do you think you're doing?"

She didn't even look at him. Her gaze seared the crowd at his back. Instinctively, he raised his head to see what had caused the flash of fear that darkened her lively blue eyes. He was still surveying the crowd when without warning she turned back to him and stretched up on her toes. Clasping his face, she tugged it down to within inches of her own.

"Please help me."

At least, that's what he thought she said. Then her lips covered his, whisper-soft and tasting of champagne. Her hands delved beneath the tuxedo's jacket and slid around his waist. Her enticingly feminine body arched boldly against him.

The unexpected kiss was urgent, lacking all trace of finesse. Reckless, almost frantic, her lips moved against his mouth. His shock and annoyance faded under the impact.

Her lips were incredibly soft.

The warm, velvety feel stirred an instant, unanticipated reaction. He took control of the kiss without making a conscious decision. Slowly he moved his mouth over hers in a gentle but insistent demand. Her lips parted in surprise. Roderick slid one broad hand beneath the threads of her long, silky hair and cupped the back of her head to deepen the kiss. She froze.

He'd meant to shock her, but he found himself strangely reluctant to let her go. He allowed himself another brief moment to trace the outline of her mouth with his tongue. Startled eyes opened in alarm. Bright crystal blue, they held his gaze as she stood rigidly in his arms. Her breath felt warm against his skin even as Roderick nibbled gently on her bottom lip. He was mildly astonished when she made no effort to pull free of his embrace.

"What are you doing?"

Her breathy words sounded puzzled rather than angry. Amusement carved a reluctant smile. "No woman's ever had to ask me that question before."

The expression that flitted across her features was hard to define and gone in an instant. She dropped her hands from his body.

"I wouldn't have thought someone so practiced would

need to have his ego stroked," she said with just the slightest hitch in her voice.

Roderick raised his eyebrows letting his enjoyment show. "Ah, but they do say practice makes perfect."

She tilted her head to one side. "Uh-huh. If you find a way to market all that practice, you could be a wealthy man one day."

He found himself wanting to tell her that he already was a wealthy man and it had nothing to do with his ability to kiss, but discretion stopped him in time. Before he could think of another suitable response, an inebriated man bumped into them. Roderick gripped her arms through the soft fur of the coat to steady her. The man muttered what was probably an apology and kept going. The fascinating young woman looked pointedly down at Roderick's hand. Only then did he release his hold on the fur.

She took another step back and her gaze swiftly darted about the crowd before she trained those amazing eyes back on him.

"I have to leave. If it wouldn't be too much trouble, do you think you could walk me out?"

It hit him then. She was scared. Oh, she had it under tight control, but fear nipped at the edges of her features. Tension pleated her brow as her gaze slid about the room again.

What was she afraid of? Several possibilities came to mind. Intrigued, Roderick resisted an impulse to follow her gaze.

"Could we hurry?" she demanded breathlessly.

He allowed a quick glance around even as he amazed both of them by tugging her against his side. "All right. Let's go."

"Thanks. I'll give you the coat back when we get out of here."

Who was she? What was she doing here?

With his coat thrown over one arm, he held her firmly in place and began to escort her toward the nearby exit, still sheathed in Shereen's sable fur. Since the music was still playing, it was unlikely that Shereen would miss him for the few minutes it would take to escort this woman down to the lobby.

She was so much shorter than Shereen that the fur trailed nearly to the floor. She had to move with care to avoid tripping over the hem, but somehow the coat failed to look ludicrous on her—even though it didn't match her lighter brown hair.

No, not brown, but not quite auburn, either. There were appealing glimpses of red and gold highlights where the overhead chandeliers created glints among the long, curling strands. Most of her hair had been pulled back from her face to cascade down her back, but several strands had escaped, giving her a delightfully tousled look. She'd pulled the sides up and back, holding the hair in place with a simple iridescent green clip. Inexpensive plastic, he noted as she dodged around a crowd that blocked the main exit.

She didn't belong here.

What was she doing in this room full of wealthy movers and shakers? Security was supposed to be tight at the hotel, although Roderick hadn't been impressed with what he'd seen. He'd noted several ways a person could get inside without being stopped. Obviously, this woman had used one of them.

Unless she was here as a paid companion.

He found he didn't like that disturbing thought, but he couldn't stop chewing on the idea. It was the dress, of course. Too bold. Too bright. Too cheap.

No one stopped them as they left the crowded room. As

far as Roderick could tell, no one was paying them any attention at all.

"Amorous boyfriend?" he asked quietly.

She didn't respond. He wasn't sure she had heard him.

The mezzanine was filled with the overflow from the party. As the loud music faded, his nervous companion continued to dart glances at the crowd as they moved with subtle haste among the revelers. Her agitation was more palpable now. Roderick felt his own senses coming sharply alert. She moved briskly, taking two quick steps to every one of his longer strides. He sensed she was barely restraining a desire to break into a run.

"Would you like me to slow down?" he asked.

"No!"

"Stay cool," he advised at this sharp reaction. "No one is watching us."

She turned a fragile, heart-shaped face up to his in surprise. He had the distinct impression that on some level she'd all but dismissed his presence despite the arm he still had around her shoulders. Roderick could honestly say he wasn't used to being dismissed by anyone, much less a woman he had just kissed. He tamped down an indignant spurt of annoyance. She'd asked for his help. The least she could do was show a little gratitude.

"Not the elevators," she said impatiently, nudging him away from the press of people waiting before the slow-moving glass cages.

He didn't blame her. He preferred the escalators himself, but probably not for the same reason. As he guided her through the throng, she lifted her face and offered him an unexpected smile.

"Thank you."

Roderick inhaled sharply. She certainly wasn't a

beauty—nothing like Shereen. Her face was too narrow, her chin almost pointy, and those incredibly clear blue eyes were too wide, lending her face a quizzical look. But that smile of hers lit her features and changed everything. A man would overlook any number of flaws to see a smile like that.

"You're welcome."

She also had gorgeous skin. Shereen spent long hours in front of a mirror trying to achieve the natural, healthy glow that emanated from this slip of a woman. Roderick would bet half his considerable fortune that she had done nothing more to enhance her appearance than to apply lipstick and some eyeliner.

Most of the bright red lipstick had been chewed away, but a telltale hint remained. The thin line of eyeliner had smudged, adding to a waiflike appearance that was strangely appealing.

Because he found himself studying her so closely, he noticed the thin white line at her hairline. The scar was tiny, really. Easily overlooked since it disappeared into her carelessly styled long hair. Still, that jagged line of imperfection was a close match to a scar he carried. His jaw tightened as he remembered the cause of his scar and he wondered how she had come by hers.

"It isn't every day a man has a chance to play Sir Galahad to a lady in distress," he told her. Cynically, he had to admit he was sort of enjoying the role. But he couldn't help wondering exactly what—or whom—he was rescuing her from.

"You're doing a great job," she told him, barely glancing up as her gaze continued to rove restlessly.

Roderick frowned. "Do you have a name?"

"Of course I do."

As they stepped onto the descending escalator she hesitated, sending another quick look over her shoulder. Roderick turned back, as well. No one so much as glanced their way. As he withdrew his hand from her shoulder, he gave it a comforting pat. She raised dark sooty lashes to study him.

"Sorry. I do appreciate your help," she told him earnestly.

Mollified, Roderick inclined his head politely, ignoring a renewed stirring of sexual interest. She wasn't flirting or playing coy, which was just as well. She was not his type. Yet she intrigued him, and he'd have to give her high marks for her ability to think on her feet—not to mention that she didn't seem the least bit unnerved by him or his size.

"You didn't answer my question," he pointed out.

"No, I didn't."

Obviously, she didn't intend to identify herself or explain this desperate flight. Roderick's gaze skated to her fingers. Like the rest of her, her hand was small and well shaped. The nails were cropped unfashionably short and were adorned by brilliant scarlet nail polish. He found the color annoyed him the same way his brief glimpse of her daring dress had done. Somehow, neither one belonged on her.

He could only see her right hand, because the other one was lost in the folds of the coat pulled so tightly around her. To conceal the bright color of her dress, he decided. She wore no jewelry other than a pair of inexpensive crystal earrings. Once again he wondered what she had been doing there. The tickets had been pricey by any standards. *Was* she a paid escort?

He didn't like the idea, but it wouldn't go away. She didn't have the hardened, jaded look he would have expected from a professional, but then, what did he know? He'd never had the need to hire a companion.

"Am I in danger of being accosted by an angry husband?"

Those soft lips curved with humor. "Worried?"

"Not particularly," he replied, affronted. "I was curious."

He was rewarded by the flash of that dazzling smile again.

"No husband."

As they moved carefully onto the next set of moving stairs he told himself her situation was really none of his business. He didn't want or need to be involved in her problem, but her caginess was becoming annoying.

She teetered a bit, shifting her stance carefully as she tugged at the trailing coat. For the first time Roderick noticed the height of the glittery green shoes she wore. He was pretty sure the bold color matched her dress.

"You're going to break your neck in those things if you aren't careful," he warned. The heels were slender needles of stupidity. Why she didn't simply teeter out of them was beyond his comprehension.

Once again her ready smile flickered to life. "You could be right. They certainly pinch like the devil."

He suppressed an answering smile and added spunk to her other attributes. "Why don't you take them off?"

"My feet would get cold," she said reasonably. "Besides, I'd trip over the hem of this coat. Your lady must be a giant."

His lips tightened at the reminder of Shereen. If by some chance she had returned to the table and missed him, she would not be in the best of moods when he made it back upstairs. On the other hand, she wouldn't lack for a partner to take her back out on the dance floor.

"On the contrary," he told the woman. "Shereen's the perfect size for a model."

"Ah, that explains it."

"Explains what?" he asked, curious despite himself.

She gave him another of those disarming smiles and shook her head without responding.

Sanity belatedly surfaced. He knew nothing about this puff of a woman. She could be running from the police for all he knew.

"You weren't an invited guest, were you?"

She tipped back her head to regard him, humor glinting in her eyes.

"What gave me away, the lack of diamonds?"

"Among other things."

"Maybe I find all that flash and dazzle boringly overdone."

"You're a woman," he told her flatly. "Don't pretend to be so cynical."

"Chauvinist. I wouldn't dream of it. You've already perfected that role."

Stunned, he watched her step onto the last leg of the escalator. The heavy coat nearly tripped her this time. Roderick steadied her. She nodded her thanks as a subtle awareness hovered between them. He didn't want to admit it, but she fascinated him.

"I hope you and your lady weren't in a terrible hurry to get home. I'd hate to think I delayed you."

"No. Shereen's apartment isn't far from here."

"That's good. Thank you, again."

She wasn't ignoring him now, but wariness had crept in around the edges of her expression. Roderick released the coat and her arm, unsettled by his reluctance to do so.

"You're welcome, again. I'll drive you home."

He wasn't sure who was more surprised, the woman, or himself. Shereen was probably fuming by now. Or, he conceded more honestly, still dancing with one of her many conquests. They were with a large, boisterous group of acquaintances after all. Still, he couldn't drive off and leave her there. He needed to go back up and fetch her. First, he'd have the valet bring his car around so his mystery woman could wait inside safely. Shereen would be furious, of course, but even she would see that they couldn't just leave her at this hour of the night.

Where was her coat? Still upstairs? He could bring it down with Shereen. But before he could voice these thoughts, the two of them reached the expansive lobby. The woman stepped forward briskly, turned and slid out of the heavy fur. Lifting up on tiptoes, she placed a chaste kiss on his chin.

Once more, she'd caught him unprepared. Roderick wasn't used to being surprised. Things generally went as he planned them. At least they had until she'd waltzed into his life. As she drew away he realized there was no artificial odor of perfume or other fragrance on her skin.

"Thanks again, hero. I'm not what you think I am, but I did need rescuing. Happy New Year."

"Wait!"

But she didn't wait. She dropped the heavy coat and stepped away. Automatically, Roderick caught the fur before it hit the ground. She hurried off without a backward glance, heels clattering against the marbled floor.

Roderick had every intention of pursuing her, but stunned, he found his brain still focused on the absurd bit of material she called a dress. There wasn't much fabric involved. The high mandarin collar and long sleeves were the garment's deceptive concession to modesty. The keyhole effect in front was so low she looked in immediate danger of disaster.

And she was built perfectly for disaster. For such a petite woman, she was incredibly full and lush. The bodice snugged her body like a layer of glittery green skin before it flared out from her waist to swirl about slender, well-shaped calves. It appeared she wasn't wearing a thing under that dress because in back, the fabric was missing clear down to her coccyx.

"I'm not what you think I am."

He wasn't sure what he thought she was, but the word *stripper* boldly came to mind. Certainly that clingy, sparkly material begged to be stripped from her enticing form.

Roderick was irritated to find himself aroused. He curbed the impulse to chase after her and demand answers. The lady was a mass of contradictions. That sweetly innocent smile did not go with that dress.

But the body did.

He muttered a low oath. One hand returned to massage his temple as he watched her step outside. He'd managed to forget his headache while he'd been with her, but now it returned with a vengeance. Beyond the plate-glass windows of the lobby, snow billowed in the wind. It wasn't merely snowing, it was snowing hard. And all he could think was that there was very little of anything covering all that soft bare skin.

With a curse, he strode after her. He reached the double glass doors just in time to see the bellman shut the door of a taxicab.

Roderick paused. The cab would have a heater. She wouldn't freeze. Obviously she had somewhere to go—someplace private, no doubt—and he did not want to think about watching her strip away that clingy bit of fabric.

Roderick shook his head at the disquieting train of thought. Who cared what the woman did with her nights? Hooker, stripper, paid companion…there were plenty of lost souls in Washington, D.C.

With a growl, he started back across the concourse to the escalator. He wasn't sure why he was angry, or why her departure left him feeling so dejected. It made no difference who she was running away from. He had problems of his own, not the least of which was getting Shereen to agree to leave the party before midnight so he could go home and relax.

Going up the escalator, he attempted to push the stranger from his thoughts. The unsettling imp would have to fend for herself. She'd already demonstrated an uncanny ability to do just that. There was no reason for concern to jab at him. Nevertheless, he couldn't help comparing the past few minutes to the ridiculous fairy tale his sister had been so fond of as a child.

So this was how the prince had felt when the clock had struck twelve. And while Roderick would hardly consider himself a prince, the only thing missing had been the glass slipper.

Chapter Two

Melanie Andrews waited for the driver to repeat the address in heavily accented English before she settled back against the seat of the smelly cab with a hard shiver. The vehicle would have been plenty warm if she'd been wearing a coat, or even decent clothing, but she wasn't. She thought longingly of her warm cloth coat, still inside the luxury suite on the top floor of the hotel. The coat was old, but still serviceable. Too bad she'd never see it again.

She met the driver's expression in the rearview mirror. He smiled broadly and winked. She narrowed her eyes and gave him a hostile glare. If he had any perverted ideas about taking her someplace besides the address she'd just given him, he'd find out exactly how valuable these stiletto heels could be. He needed to pay closer attention to the worsening road conditions.

No doubt he thought she was a hooker. That's probably what her rescuer had thought, too. This dress was enough to give anyone that impression. It was exactly the impression she'd been trying to create.

Mel sighed. She looked down at the objects in her hand and a jolt of panic tingled down her spine. She'd shoved the dead man's keys and plastic card in the deep pocket of the fur coat, but she'd only been able to palm the card before she dropped the fur because she'd also had her rescuer's wallet and keys in her hand. She was going to need those keys.

She stared at the garish club card and tried to fight the panic clawing at her. She'd taken the wrong bit of plastic. This was not the key card she'd removed from the dead man's wallet. The card to get into his office building must be still inside the fur coat. Her prints were all over that bit of plastic.

Mel forced her breathing to steady. Panic was the fast road to disaster. Her prints weren't on file anywhere and the model wouldn't know what the card was or where it had come from when she did discover the thing. She'd probably toss it out without a second thought. Besides, there was nothing Mel could do about the situation at the moment. She didn't even have a last name for the woman her rescuer had called Shereen.

Ignoring the driver's covert glances at the front of her dress, Mel opened the well-tooled leather wallet she'd palmed. Her fingers shook, and not from the cold. She hated that she'd repaid his kindness by lifting his wallet, but she'd needed to pay for the cab ride somehow. It was galling to realize that she hadn't planned as well as she should have. She should have pinned money inside her dress, or at least grabbed her purse when she fled. Not that there had been time for that. Getting away had been far more important than searching for her purse on the bed filled with coats and a dead man.

Mel knew her thoughts were darting about in a ridiculous manner, but thinking of other things was better than thinking about that horrible dead body and the fact that the D.C. police would soon be scouring the city for her.

She shook her head and stared at the driver's license in her hands. Roderick Anthony Laughlin III. There was a mouthful, yet somehow the stuffy name suited him, even if it was at odds with that kiss.

She touched a finger lightly to her lips, remembering the hot press of his mouth and the answering heat that had stirred within her. The man had almost swept her off her spiked heels. For a split second Mel had lost track of everything. That had never happened to her before. It unsettled her.

Who was Roderick Laughlin?

The picture on his driver's license didn't do him justice. His wasn't a handsome face. The shape was too angular, the features too boldly intense. Yet even in the picture, the sense of controlled power and self-assurance came through. From the balcony, she'd singled him out as much for his height as for his apparent destination. Yet according to his driver's license, Roderick Laughlin was only six feet tall. He'd seemed taller. Larger.

Safe.

How crazy was that? Claire was right. She needed to get out more. Meeting interesting men was not easy when one was stuck in a kitchen day after day.

Of course, it would be even harder to do from inside a jail cell.

Mel sighed. Roderick Laughlin's leanness had been deceptive. There had been undeniable strength in the rippled muscles she'd felt beneath that perfectly fitted tuxedo jacket. Why was it men always looked so appealing in a tuxedo?

Mel shook aside that thought. Her slight frame tended to give some men the mistaken belief she needed to be shielded and protected. She was willing to use that impression when it suited her purposes, like tonight, but mostly coddling annoyed her. Roderick Laughlin hadn't annoyed her. Instead he'd made her sharply aware of her femininity.

That had been some kiss.

Mel yanked her thoughts from that path, too, and flipped to the compartment holding his money. The unanticipated wad of bills made her bite her lower lip to stifle a gasp of dismay. Didn't the man believe in banks and credit cards?

Wryly, she wondered what she had expected. A bash like the one at that fancy hotel catered only to the rich and famous. Apparently, Roderick Laughlin was rich. How unfortunate that he chose to carry around enough cash to send her to jail for grand theft if she was caught.

She nearly laughed out loud. Grand theft was the least of her worries. The police would be far more interested in tagging her for murder than a simple lift.

"Blast!"

"You say something lady?" the driver asked.

"No!"

His stare was just this side of a leer as they stopped for a traffic light. Mel met his gaze coldly in the rearview mirror until he lowered his eyes.

Good. She did not need another problem tonight.

The evening had not gone well. At first she'd stayed close to the group she'd come in with. Then she'd spotted Harold DiAngelis across the room. She was sure she'd seen a flash of startled recognition in his eyes before she'd moved away in search of her quarry.

Except he shouldn't have known who she was.

DiAngelis worked with Gary, but her brother didn't like the older man. The two had never socialized. Heck, they barely spoke, from what she gathered. There was no way Gary would have mentioned her to DiAngelis.

There hadn't been time to wonder about that then, but she was fretting over it now. DiAngelis was bound to identify her to the police. His presence at the hotel at that particular party couldn't be coincidence. Was DiAngelis somehow involved in the theft of her brother's program? Maybe he was even the person who had killed Carl Boswell and taken the DVD!

The taxi slid on the slick pavement as they rounded a corner. The driver swore fluently. He barely avoided a collision with a stretch of parked cars. He offered her a wink and a wide grin as he straightened out and double-parked in front of a tired-looking redbrick building.

Mel handed him the money she'd pulled from the wallet in anticipation.

"Want company?" the driver asked, his leer firmly in place.

Mel inclined her head toward the lighted window of the apartment three stories up. Even from inside the cab the sounds of a party in full swing were unmistakable.

"I've already got plenty of company," she said as she handed him the money.

The man nodded acceptance, but he waited, watching her climb the stone steps to the entrance before he roared off to disappear into the swirling snowflakes. As soon as the cab was out of sight, Mel went back down and hurried along the sidewalk as fast as her borrowed too-high heels would allow.

Snow peppered her skin. In minutes she was liberally coated from her hair to the pinching points of her shoes where her frozen toes begged for mercy. She was so cold she wasn't sure how she made it to the Metro parking lot where she'd left her car earlier.

The police would trace the cab, of course, but the building would bring them to a dead end. Now, if only she could get her reluctant engine to start! Her twelve-year-old car did not like the cold any more than she did, and the transmission was going.

Curbing her frantic need to get away from the area, Mel finally coaxed the engine to life while shivers wracked her. Nothing resembling heat came from the vents even after she pulled out of the subway parking lot. The streets were growing more treacherous by the minute. Mel didn't have to turn on the radio to know a snow emergency ban would be in effect. That meant she'd have to find a parking place near her apartment building on one of the side streets that wasn't deemed an emergency route. Too bad she couldn't afford the monthly fee to park in the parking garage a block over.

By the time she reached the foyer of her apartment building, two horrifically long blocks from where she'd had to park, the new year was several minutes old and she could no longer feel the finger that pressed Claire Bradshaw's apartment buzzer.

"Yes?" the tinny voice questioned over the speaker.

"Claire, it's Mel. Let me in."

The buzzer answered her plea. Teeth chattering uncontrollably, she grasped the door handle and pushed eagerly into the warmth of the foyer. Her skin burned with returning circulation as she climbed the three flights and tried to ignore the icy rivulets of water melting against her skin.

"Good Lord'a'mighty have mercy," Claire exclaimed as Mel reached her floor, huffing between fierce shivers. "What on earth were you doing running around outside dressed like that?"

"Tempting frostbite," she managed.

Claire tsk-tsked as she ushered Mel inside. "Where's your coat? Never mind. Get inside before you drop."

Her elderly neighbor ushered her into a cozy warm room. Mel heard her suck in another gasp as she got a good view of Mel's backside.

"Good Lord," Claire whispered. "Didn't I tell you that dress was overkill?"

Another time, Mel might have laughed. Claire had told her as much, even though she'd only seen the dress on the hanger until now.

"I didn't have a lot of choice. Sue has flamboyant taste." A serious understatement. Sue had been Mel's next-door neighbor when she first moved to D.C. Outgoing and courageous, the pretty redhead had made it impossible for Mel not to be friends with her despite how little they had in common. But her friend was exactly her size right down to the shoe size. There hadn't been time to go shopping for something more suitable after Gary called so she'd stopped at her friend's apartment to borrow an outfit for the party.

Fortunately, Claire hadn't lived some seventy-odd years without learning when to give in to shock and when to get on with what needed doing.

"Into the shower," she ordered. "You'll have pneumonia if we don't get you warmed up."

"No time."

Claire Bradshaw scowled. Without bothering to argue she went to the closet and plucked out a heavy cardigan sweater and helped Mel into the thick wool. Forcing her down into the nearest chair, her friend quickly wrapped the afghan from the couch around her legs.

Lethargy pulled at her. Mel shut her eyes and allowed herself a minute to huddle in the chair, absorbing warmth into her chilled, damp body. When Claire set a steaming cup of hot chocolate on the end table at her elbow, Mel forced her eyes open again.

"Drink every drop," Claire ordered. "Hot chocolate warms a body faster than anything else."

Mel tried to pick up the mug, but her hands shook too much to hold the heavy stoneware. Claire's wrinkled face added new creases as she lifted the mug so Mel could take a sip. The liquid was hot but not scalding, and Mel drank greedily. The next time she told her hands to reach for the cup, they closed around the blessed warmth and she shuddered gratefully.

A moment later Claire produced a fluffy warm towel. She must have taken it from the small clothes dryer in her kitchen because the terry cloth was soothingly warm and smelled of fabric softener.

"Use this on your hair."

Mel sank her hands into the thick towel with a sigh of pleasure.

"I don't have much time," she told her friend as she toweled her sodden hair.

"The police?" Claire asked quietly.

Mel grimaced. "I'm afraid so."

"Did you get the disk?" Claire asked with a nod at the wallet and key case Mel had dropped on the end table.

Mel shook her head, feeling the bitter weight of defeat. "It's a DVD, not a disk, and no. Someone beat me to it."

"Oh, dear. What can I do?"

"I need the spare key to get inside my apartment. My key is in my coat pocket and I had to leave it behind. I have to disappear for a few days."

"The wallet?"

Used to her friend's verbal shorthand, Mel had no trouble understanding that question. "That isn't the reason. The wallet didn't come from that party."

"You went to another party?"

"Not by choice."

She picked up the supple leather, allowing her finger-tips to stroke the soft, expensive-looking material. Claire raised questioning eyebrows and Mel lifted her shoulders trying not to think about the handsome stranger who had helped her escape.

"Carl Boswell was murdered before I got there."

"Oh, my."

"It gets worse. The program was gone and someone Gary works with was at the party. Harold DiAngelis. I'm pretty sure he recognized me. I caught him staring at me."

Claire snorted and looked meaningfully down at her dress.

Mel managed a weak smile. "I wish it *had* been the dress, but I'm not even sure he noticed what I was wearing."

Claire raised expressive eyebrows.

"Really. It's no coincidence he was there, Claire. I'm betting he killed Boswell and took the program."

"Large assumption."

"Maybe, but you know how Gary feels about DiAngelis."

"How would he know about Gary's program?"

"How did he know who I am?" Reluctantly, she pushed aside the blanket and unwound the towel from her head. "I'd better go. DiAngelis is sure to put the police on to me."

"Where's your purse?"

"I dropped it on the bed when I searched Boswell."

"You searched him?"

Mel shivered at the memory. At the time, she hadn't let herself think about what she was doing. She didn't want to think about it now, either.

"Where's your coat?"

"I had to leave it and Sue's purse behind."

"Mel!"

"I wasn't carrying ID, not that it matters now. But I do owe Sue a new purse. I need to go."

"You'd be safe here," Claire protested.

"I don't think so. If DiAngelis recognized me, there's no telling what he knows about the people connected to Gary. He may know about you, as well. Pull the shades, turn out the lights, and don't answer the door or the phone, whatever you do."

Mel rose to her feet, feeling woozy and more tired than she would have liked. She was still chilled and damp but her instincts were screaming at her to get moving. Claire bustled back to the kitchen and returned with Mel's spare key.

"Where will you go?" she asked.

Once again, Mel rubbed the supple leather of the wallet. "I have a bolt-hole in mind. Don't worry."

"At my age, worrying is an art form."

Mel smiled and started to remove the sweater. The older woman shook her gray curls.

"Later. Do what you have to, Mel. I'm here if I can help."

"You already have."

Mel hugged her friend. For just a second, she let herself inhale the older woman's familiar powdery scent. Claire had once been her grandmother's best friend. Now she was Mel's.

"I don't know what I'd do without you."

Claire issued another ladylike snort. "You'd manage. You're like your parents."

"Not Grandma?"

Claire smiled. "She'd be proud of you."

"Not after tonight's debacle," Mel said ruefully, "but thanks again, Claire. Oh, and happy New Year."

"Stay safe."

"That's the plan."

Mel was still smiling as she let herself inside the dark apartment across the hall. Without light, she crossed to the bedroom and began collecting what she needed. She pulled a pair of sweatpants from the dresser drawer and tugged them on over the dress. She couldn't afford to leave the dress behind and she didn't want to waste time removing it. Moving fast, despite the shivers plaguing her, Mel struggled into a baggy black sweatshirt that barely fit over the cumbersome sweater. The result was restrictive, but seductively warm.

She found heavy cotton socks by touch in another drawer before she reached for the shoe tree to feel for her black sneakers. Snatching underwear at random, she fumbled for the old scuffed duffel bag shoved in the back of her closet and stuffed it with the rest of the essential items.

Because she'd been listening hard the whole time, the anticipated sound of a car pulling up outside sent her rushing across the room to peer down at the sidewalk. Two men exited a long sedan that had pulled to the curb. They peered up at the building through the hurling snowflakes.

Mel knew they couldn't see her, but she remained perfectly still anyhow until they looked away and mounted the steps. She was out of time.

Tossing the tennis shoes on top, she closed the bag, jammed her feet into black steel-toed work boots, grabbed her only other jacket and raced for the door. Claire's buzzer shrilled. Hers a moment later. No doubt they were buzzing at random in hopes someone would let them inside. Sooner or later someone would.

Mel took time to lace her boots and relock her front door before sprinting down the hall to the laundry room at the far end. It took muscle, but she finally got the frozen window open. Tossing her coat and the bag to the ground, she climbed onto the narrow snow-covered ledge that circled the third floor. She maneuvered the window down until it snapped closed and wished she'd taken the time to pull the gloves from her coat pocket. Her fingers cooperated despite feeling numb as she worked her way along the ledge to the drainpipe. Testing the give, she found it still anchored securely. Using the pipe she worked her way down the side of the building.

A foot from the bottom, she kicked free and dropped. The wind had picked up, so snow would cover her tracks quickly. She scooped up her belongings and melted into the shadows of the neighboring building.

RODERICK WAS NOT in a good mood when he returned to the main ballroom. Shereen stood near the dance floor in animated conversation with Roderick's most powerful competitor and that rarest of species—a wealthy, eligible bachelor like himself.

"Roderick!" Shereen greeted him when she spotted him. "Just look at my dress! It's completely ruined! Some clumsy drunk dumped an entire glass of burgundy all over me! I don't know what I'm going to do. I tried wiping the stains off in the bathroom, but I'm sure my dry cleaner will never be able to get them out completely."

"Then it's a good thing I brought your coat," he told her.

Her perfectly plucked eyebrows arched. "You want to leave? Now?"

"It isn't even midnight yet," Larry Wilhelm protested.

"Wilhelm," Roderick acknowledged the other man grudgingly.

"Don't mind Roderick, he has a headache," Shereen said with asperity. "I suggested he go take another aspirin or have another drink, but Roderick isn't fond of parties, are you darling?"

"No," he said tersely.

Deliberately, Wilhelm ran a knuckle down Shereen's bare upper arm. "You know what they say about all business and no play, Laughlin."

Shereen offered him a teasing smile. Roderick didn't bother to conceal his annoyance with the pair. "I prefer to do my playing in private."

Wilhelm raised his eyebrows mockingly. "Sorry, Laughlin, I didn't realize I was treading on private property."

The heck he didn't.

"I am hardly anyone's property," Shereen stated archly.

Looking at the haughty arrogance in every line of her elegant body, Roderick realized how little he actually liked the woman underneath those superficial charms. Shereen was decorative and intelligent and extremely talented in the bedroom, but the world was filled with women like her. While they had suited each other for a surprising number of months now, he realized the relationship was no longer worth the effort.

Had he come to that realization because of Shereen's apparent interest in Wilhelm, or because of a small, pointy face and two large eyes that had lit with an inner glow whenever that brilliant smile appeared?

It was an understatement to say the young woman he'd just helped wasn't his type. She was short rather than statuesque, and far from model thin. And heaven knew she had no sense of style. Still, she intrigued him, and Roderick had always enjoyed a good puzzle.

"That was rather rude, darling," Shereen told him as he led her away. "Larry was simply being nice by keeping me company while I waited for you."

He didn't have a chance to voice his opinion on that because just then the mayor and his wife flagged them down. Being rude to Wilhelm was one thing, but Roderick genuinely liked the young mayor and the group of people they were with. Shereen drifted away, leaving him sorely tempted to let her find her own way home. Good manners prevailed and they stayed until midnight after all. By the time he got Shereen out of the ballroom and onto the escalator, his headache was creeping close to migraine territory.

"...and I don't know why we couldn't take the elevator," Shereen was complaining. "Escalators are so dirty."

"Too crowded," he told her shortly.

"This aversion you have for elevators is really quite annoying at times, you know that?"

He paused to regard her before crossing to the next set of moving steps. "If you want to take the elevator, Shereen, feel free," he told her brusquely and turned away.

"You really are in a mood, aren't you?" Shereen said waspishly as she hurried after him. "You're still miffed because I was talking to Larry earlier. You know, just because you and Larry often find yourselves rivals at times, it wouldn't have hurt you to make nice. Larry does move in all the right circles, you know. He was just telling me how his company got a juicy new contract working with Homeland Security. Instead of acting so rudely, you'd do well to encourage a relationship with him."

Roderick didn't look at her. "I'll leave that to you."

She inhaled audibly.

"Don't tell me you were jealous, darling," she purred after a moment.

"I won't."

He stepped off the escalator and moved across the tiled foyer ahead of her to hand the valet his parking ticket. Outside, snow had coated the roads, continuing its downward spiral with growing speed.

"I didn't realize," Shereen said in her most conciliatory tone of voice. "You were probably bidding on the same contract."

Roderick didn't bother to respond. She'd realized. They'd even discussed his plans. When RAL had bid on the contract and lost, he'd simply chalked it up to part of doing business. The loss had nothing to do with his instinctive dislike of the man.

Shereen fell silent beside him as they waited for the Mercedes to be brought around. Roderick barely noticed her. He was busy planning the phone call he would make first thing tomorrow morning to begin his search for the mystery woman. Anticipation had his thoughts moving briskly as the dark green sedan rolled to a stop. Roderick reached for his billfold.

And came up empty.

"Is something wrong?" Shereen asked.

"My wallet seems to be missing." He checked the other pocket. Empty, as well. Not just his wallet, his keys were gone, as well.

Shereen frowned. "Maybe it fell out in your car," she suggested. "When did you have it last?"

Roderick knew exactly when he'd had it last. He'd tipped the cloakroom attendant and replaced the wallet in his inner pocket. Then the mystery woman in the sparkly green dress had slid her arms around him—beneath the tuxedo jacket.

He swore out loud. The little witch had lifted his wallet and his keys and he'd never felt a thing. He couldn't believe he'd been suckered by a pro.

"You could have dropped it upstairs. Maybe you left it at the table. We could go back up and have a look around."

For someone who hadn't wanted to leave a minute ago, she didn't sound enthusiastic at the prospect of going back upstairs.

"I didn't lose it upstairs," he said tersely. Well, he had, but not in the way she meant. No wonder the little imp had been looking around so frantically. He wondered how many other men in the ballroom were going to find their faces red this evening.

"Are you going to call security?"

"No," he said absently. "I know exactly what happened to it." And he was generally such an excellent judge of character. "Would you mind tipping the man for me?"

Roderick was more annoyed than embarrassed to admit that he'd been suckered. He should have known better, of course, but she was a pro—and not the sort he'd thought. Well, hadn't she told him she wasn't what he'd thought?

The irony wasn't lost on him. Roderick thought about calling the police, but he knew he wouldn't and not just because he'd look foolish. He preferred to deal with the little pickpocket himself. Someone else might report her, of course, but it was a chance he was willing to take. She didn't know it, but she'd handed him the perfect excuse to find her. And he would. She'd made it easy by taking a taxi. Taxi's kept records.

"You're in a perfectly foul mood this evening, you know that?" Shereen asked as he pulled carefully out into traffic.

"I suppose I am."

Wisely, she fell silent, leaving him to concentrate on the

road. His thoughts were busy conjuring up mock conversations with the imp when he located her. His imagination was enjoying the exercise when Shereen turned toward him again.

"I am sorry, darling," she offered, laying a long-fingered hand on his thigh. "I didn't appreciate how severe your headache must be. I guess you had a beastly night. I'll make it up to you when we get to my place."

"Save it, Shereen. You made your point earlier. Consider it taken. Right now I need to concentrate."

She stiffened and withdrew. He could feel her amber eyes studying him in the glow of the dash lights, but he kept his focus on the road. The windshield wipers struggled to keep up with the falling snow.

They drove in tense silence until they reached her apartment complex. Instead of pulling into the parking garage as usual, he drove to the front of the building and stopped.

"Darling, I realize you're annoyed with me and I'm sorry. I wasn't really flirting with your archenemy, you know. Why don't you come in and let me make it up to you? It's far too treacherous to drive all the way into Virginia tonight."

Her hand moved to his thigh and stroked upward.

"Goodbye, Shereen."

The hand stopped moving and she frowned. "Pouting is most unbecoming."

"So is using sex to get your own way."

She recoiled instantly.

"Happy New Year," he added sarcastically.

The flash of anger in her expression came and went so fast he barely had time to notice. She laid a placating hand on his sleeve, her frown of concern so patently phony he had to force his arm to be still.

"We'll talk in the morning when you're feeling better."

"Don't plan on it, Shereen."

Her eyes widened as she studied his features. "You're dumping me? You are! Why you arrogant bastard!"

Without another word, she exited the car. The slamming of the door shook loose a clump of snow from the roof. Manfully, the wipers struggled to cope as it cascaded over the windshield.

Roderick pulled away without a backward glance. He generally used more finesse when breaking off relationships, but he suspected subtlety would have been wasted on Shereen. He also suspected at least some of her anger was more for show than anything else. If he wasn't mistaken, Shereen had already selected his replacement. Wilhelm's pockets better be as deep as reported if he was planning to be the next in line to woo the beautiful model. Shereen didn't come cheap.

The snowplows and salt trucks were operating with almost negligible results. The drive to her apartment had taken longer than it did in rush hour, and what was normally a fifteen- to twenty-minute trip to his place took nearly two nerve-wrenching hours as the weather continued to worsen. His headache was truly wicked by the time he pulled into his garage.

Roderick used the spare house key concealed there to let himself into the town house. As he switched the security panel back on for the night, he gave himself a mental reminder to change the code and have the door locks rekeyed. Shereen had both and could let herself in at any time. Fortunately, he didn't have to worry about that tonight.

His headache was reaching migraine proportions by the time he kicked off his dress shoes and crossed to the stairs.

He was tired. All he wanted was a hot shower and a soft bed.

He had nearly reached the upstairs hall when a sudden prickle traveled up his back to lodge at the base of his skull. Roderick stopped moving.

There was no sound out of place. No trace of smoke. The only thing he smelled was the lingering scent of nail polish remover and the bath salts Shereen favored.

Yet something was wrong.

Adrenaline replaced his headache and exhaustion. At thirty-two, he knew better than to ignore his instincts. He backed down the steps quietly.

One touch of the button on the control panel would bring the police and a security team, but he'd feel worse than a fool if he brought anyone out on a night like this and the house was empty. His security system was state-of-the-art technology. By checking the panel he could see at a glance if the system had been breached. It should have alerted him if that had been the case, even if his sister had stopped by for some reason, but it hadn't.

Was it possible that he was suddenly developing an imagination?

Not hardly. The thief had taken his house keys along with his identification. No doubt that had raised subconscious alarms. She couldn't use the keys to get inside without tripping the alarm, yet the sense of wrongness persisted.

Roderick made his way to the softly glowing panel and ran a diagnostic check. The system recorded no entry prior to his, but it did show a momentary interrupt in power a couple of hours ago. A power surge or a flicker in the house current? It hadn't lasted long enough to trip his pager and alert him, yet his unease remained.

The only sound inside the house was the ticking of the huge grandfather clock in the living room. He checked the doors and windows. All secure. His senses weren't placated.

Roderick abhorred guns, and a knife wasn't a particularly efficient form of defense against an unknown assailant, but he wanted something in his hand before he went upstairs again. Moving to the kitchen, he crossed the tiles in his stocking feet and quietly removed a heavy skillet. Hefting it, he tested its weight. He was tired and irritable and feeling oddly theatric, but this was his home. If someone had gotten past the system somehow, they were going to regret the action.

He strode to the staircase and promptly stumbled over the shoes he'd left at the bottom. He kept himself from falling, but he'd just lost the element of surprise if someone else was inside.

Jaw set, pan swinging, Roderick mounted the steps by twos. At the top he hit the wall switch. A stream of slightly yellow illumination cast shadows on the walls. Nothing else moved. There was no sound.

He turned toward the master bedroom. The double doors yawned wide-open the way he'd left them, yet he entered cautiously. At first glance nothing appeared disturbed. He moved toward the closet and froze. Heart-pounding adrenaline shot through his system. If he hadn't taken off his shoes downstairs he would never have felt the dampness.

Someone had walked across the carpeting with wet feet.

He gripped the pan firmly while his heart tried to drill through his chest. His palms slicked with sweat. He gazed about slowly. The bedroom was empty. So was the spacious walk-in closet.

He crossed to the master bath. The large room was a hedonistic delight. The tub sprawled on a raised dais, twice as wide and half again as long and deep as a normal tub. Jets were built into the sides so it could be operated as a whirlpool. A sinfully appealing skylight loomed overhead and there was a separate, oversized shower with multiple heads so that water could run freely over a person from both sides—or two people could share as he and Shereen had done on more than one occasion.

An enormous double vanity filled the far wall with mirrored glass. The glass was partially fogged. His blurred image stared back at him.

Running a quick finger over the inside of the tub he discovered it had been wiped but was still damp. The unmistakable scent of Shereen's favorite bath oil mingled in the air along with the odor of nail polish remover. That was what his subconscious had tried to alert him to when he started up the stairs. Those odors shouldn't have been there. Shereen hadn't used the large bathroom in more than a week.

He strode back to the bedroom. This time when he surveyed the room, he did so slowly, taking in small details. His muscles contracted the moment he spotted his wallet and key case on the tall dresser. Roderick didn't need to open the expensive leather. It seemed inevitable that his money would all be inside.

He lowered the pan. Red-stained tissues were clumped in his wastebasket. Ridiculously, he was glad. The nail color had been all wrong on her. But how had the little thief gotten past his unbeatable security system?

His legs carried him to the large guest room. He slapped the wall switch. Nothing happened. The lamp on the nightstand must have been turned off at the base. It didn't matter. The light from the hall was adequate.

The first thing he saw was the sparkly green material lying in a heap on the floor.

The second thing he saw was the body on the bed.

Chapter Three

Mel awoke from a dreamless sleep to adrenaline-pumping fear. A large shadowy shape loomed over her. With a startled cry, she rolled away from the threat, off the other side of the bed to land on her feet. She crouched there poised to fight or flee while her brain attempted to assimilate what was happening.

A startled masculine oath ripped from the shadow's throat. He half raised an object in his hand defensively at her cry and Mel came all the way to consciousness as memory clicked into place. She was in the guest bedroom in the town house belonging to Roderick Laughlin III. The shadow could be no one else but her host.

Actually, as her heart continued to thud a staccato beat, she wasn't sure which of them was the more startled by the situation. She'd been taught that taking the offensive was always the best policy so she gave vent to the panic that had clawed the back of her throat.

"You idiot! You scared the heck out of me!"

He lowered the object slowly. "What?"

"You could have given me a heart attack! You should have called out or something. Don't you know you should never startle someone awake? I thought you were an intruder."

Speechless, he remained unmoving.

As her vision penetrated the darkened room, his shocked expression drained the remainder of her fear. She had no idea what time it was, but it felt very late, or very early, depending on the point of view. The house was dark and Roderick Laughlin still wore his tuxedo—right down to the perfectly knotted tie at his throat. Mostly backlit by the hall light, he stood there gripping what looked like a frying pan. The image was so ludicrous, Mel couldn't help it, she giggled.

"Sorry," she apologized quickly. "But you look ridiculous holding that skillet. Were you going to bean me over the head or did you come to offer me breakfast? Because if you're cooking, I'm eating."

His eyes blinked shut for a moment. "Oh, hell. You're a fruitcake."

"I most certainly am not!" She aimed a finger at his chest. "Listen, buddy, I'm not the one dressed in a tuxedo holding a frying pan in my guest room in the middle of the night. It is still the middle of the night, isn't it? What time is it? And what are you doing here, anyway? Shouldn't you and the model be ringing in the new year at her place all night?"

He shook his head like a fighter who'd taken one punch too many.

"How did you get in here?" he growled.

Uh-oh. Dangerous territory.

"Like any normal person. Through the front door. I, uh, sort of borrowed your keys."

This time when he shook his head, she realized he'd recovered. He'd moved beyond shock to a deadly calm.

"How did you get past my security system?"

"Oh, that," she stalled.

"Yes, that."

When no suitable answer came to mind, Mel gave what she hoped was a negligent shrug and started moving around the bed. "You need a better system."

He tensed.

"There is no better system," he gritted out. "Who the devil are you?"

"Really?" she asked dubiously even though she knew darn well what he'd said was true. She'd never come across an alarm system quite like his before. Even her father would be impressed. The dratted thing had nearly defeated her.

"Look, if it makes you feel any better, it did take me several minutes to disconnect and reconnect without tripping the interrupt circuit."

"That's impossible," he stated flatly.

Shrugging, she offered him a saucy grin. "If I were you, I'd make the company refund your money."

His voice dropped another octave. "I *own* the company that created that system."

"Oops." And didn't that just figure. Maybe she should try inserting her other foot. "Better send your people back to the drawing board."

He closed his mouth with a snap. His gaze swept her with a force that was nearly tangible. She wouldn't have thought it possible, but abruptly he tensed even further.

"Are you wearing my shirt?"

Mel pushed self-consciously at a flopping sleeve and glanced down at the white linen, thankful to see the material was draped decently to midthigh. Everything was properly covered so she tried for a wry smile.

"Sorry. I couldn't find any pajamas."

As though afraid he might be tempted to use it, he set the frying pan on the rumpled bed with exaggerated care.

"I don't wear pajamas," he said starkly.

"Yeah, that's what I figured when I couldn't find any. Normally I sleep nude, too, but I didn't feel right doing that here…you know, being a guest in your house and all."

"You are *not* a guest," he enunciated carefully. "You are a common thief."

And that raised her Irish once more. "I may be a lot of things, pal, but I am in no way *common*. And I haven't stolen a thing from you," she fired back. "I even replaced the ninety bucks I borrowed for cab fare."

"Ninety dollars! What did you do, take a tour?"

"Hey! In case you've forgotten, it's New Year's Eve."

Besides, she'd taken a series of cab rides because her car had refused to start again, but there was no point mentioning that little fact. Or how incredibly lucky she'd been to find even one cab let alone several still operating as the weather worsened.

She spread her hands. "So I was gouged, sue me. Between the holiday and the snow, I was hardly in any position to argue prices. I know I shouldn't have borrowed your wallet and your keys, but I did return them, so no harm done."

"And my shirt?"

"Oh, for crying out loud. It's the middle of the night! You want it back? Fine."

As she reached for the top button she wondered if he'd really make her take it off. Surely not. This guy was all but starched rigid. Still, the unwanted memory of their shared kiss made her usually agile fingers shake unacceptably. What if she wasn't reading him as well as she thought?

One button.

Two.

"Stop!"

Thank heavens! One more button and she'd be wishing for a belly-button ring to distract him. She waited while he muttered something under his breath and ran a hand through his hair.

"I don't believe this."

"I know what you mean," she agreed, redoing the buttons with a lot more speed than she'd managed to undo them.

Wearily, he rubbed his face. Mel noted his exhaustion and sympathized. Her own eyes felt gritty. Casting a quick glance around the room she picked up the dress that had fallen to the floor and then spotted her black sweatpants on the chair where she'd tossed them earlier.

She strode over and tugged the pants up under the shirt with faked nonchalance, conscious of his dark gaze following her every move. Given the situation, it was funny she didn't feel more threatened.

"This has been quite a night, wouldn't you say? What time is it, anyhow?"

"Past time for you to do some explaining."

Mel could hardly miss the silky threat in his quiet tone even if she hadn't noticed that the hands he'd dropped to his sides were fisted tightly.

"Who are you?" he demanded.

"That's right, we never did get around to introductions, did we? I'm Mel." Nervously she rerolled the long sleeve that kept falling down to cover her hand.

"Mel."

His lack of inflection was a rattle of warning. He regarded her with an unblinking stare as he repeated her name.

"Well, *Mel,* what are you doing in my house at…"

He glanced down at the expensive gold watch on his

wrist she'd noticed earlier. If she'd been inclined toward a life of crime that would have made a tempting target.

"...three twenty-seven in the morning? Or is it too much for me to expect a reasonable answer to that question?"

All things considered, he was taking the situation very well. He hadn't hit her with the frying pan and he wasn't reaching for the telephone to call the police.

Yet.

Mel knew it was more than she deserved. Although she was scared, she knew better than to let him see her fear.

"How come you aren't calling the police?"

"An excellent question. Should I?"

"Not on my account."

He didn't crack a smile. She watched as one of his hands went back to his forehead to rub absently. Apparently he still had a headache. Heck, she could feel the early twinges of one herself.

"Look, I really am sorry." She shrugged helplessly. "The truth is, I didn't have anywhere else to go. I was hoping you and your model would spend the night at the hotel, or at least go back to her place. I figured I could return your wallet and keys and be out of here before you showed up in the morning. I didn't expect you to come here so soon. Not in this weather."

"Why?"

"Why didn't I think you'd come back so soon?" She raised her eyebrows pointedly. "Or do you mean why didn't I have anywhere else to go?"

He started to say something, shook his head and stopped.

"Why me?" he asked flatly.

She didn't pretend to misunderstand. "You were tall and you were heading toward the exit."

He waited, but she didn't dare add anything else.

"Of course. That makes perfect sense," he said mockingly after an interminable minute had passed.

"Has anyone ever told you, you do sarcasm quite well? Look, it's late and neither of us is thinking straight right now. Why don't you go take something for your headache? I'll make us a cup of hot chocolate to help us sleep. We can finish playing twenty questions in the morning."

She moved to brush past him even though she'd known it wasn't going to be that simple. He stopped her in her tracks simply by snagging her arm. The man had a powerful grip, but she was relieved to find he knew exactly how much pressure to exert to hold her still without hurting.

"Where do you think you're going?"

Mel froze and her heart pulsed a rapid staccato. Could he see through her brave talk? Did he know how badly she was quaking inside? She was totally in the wrong here and she knew it. He had every right to call the police and have her arrested. She had to keep reminding herself that any show of fear was a weakness that might just send his hand reaching for the nearest telephone. Best to keep him off base—if she could. "To your kitchen. I could use a pain reliever myself and I can't take them on an empty stomach."

This close to him again she realized that his tuxedo still held the faintest trace of cigarette smoke and a much stronger floral perfume odor that she wasn't familiar with. The last wasn't terribly surprising since it had probably come from the girlfriend and was bound to cost more than Mel would think of spending even if she wore perfume.

Dark, tired eyes stared down at her. They mirrored his headache and exhaustion, but once again she was reminded that this was no mark. Roderick Laughlin III was a formidable adversary.

"Look, trust me," she told him, making no effort to pull away. "I'm not going anywhere dressed like this. We both need sleep."

"Trust you?"

His lips curled cynically and his eyes bored into hers.

"Interesting concept...*Mel*. Tell me why I should trust a pickpocket who dresses like a whore and enters my house illegally in the dead of the night."

Her body went rigid under the lash of his words. Before she could formulate a reply, he released her arm to rub at his eyes with the heels of his palms.

"Forget it. You've had plenty of time to strip the place bare if that was your intention. You're right. I need sleep. I do not intend to stand here talking to a crazy person at this hour of the morning."

"You know, a lesser person might take umbrage with that statement. *I,* however, will let it pass." She reached down to lift the frying pan from the bed. "Have you eaten recently? I'm thinking maybe a light omelet and some hot chocolate."

Mel started for the hall. She didn't bother to turn around to see if he was following her. The answer was not in question.

His kitchen was a dream for someone who loved to cook. Real cocoa, whole milk, even marshmallows were available in his well-stocked pantry. She started warming the milk and returned to the refrigerator.

"Oh, my. I do love a man with a well-stocked larder. Leftover ham!"

"Mel."

"And look at all these exotic cheeses! You even have fresh mushrooms and a green pepper. I may have to marry you. This is fantastic!"

"Mel," he said again from the doorway. "I'm not hungry. It's late—or rather, very early in the morning. I don't want breakfast."

"That's okay. You'll change your mind after you taste one of my omelets. I haven't eaten since—you know, I don't remember when I ate last. That means it's been far too long. That canapé I snatched earlier doesn't count as food. Nothing more than warmed cardboard with anchovies. You'd think a five-star hotel would hire better chefs. Not my problem, but it is annoying. Anyhow, we'll sleep better if we eat, trus—honest. The omelet will only take a minute and the food will help your headache. Unless…you don't suffer from migraines, do you?"

He looked affronted.

"Not normally," he said pointedly.

She tossed him a saucy grin and removed the hot milk from the burner. "Here. Stir in the cocoa while I get the omelet started."

For a minute, she thought she'd pushed him too far. Then, without a word, he took the pan from her, lifted the tin of cocoa and set about precisely measuring the powdery mix. Relieved to have passed that hurdle, Mel continued putting ingredients together.

As Roderick mixed the cocoa he wondered when he'd lost control of the situation. Then he wondered why he wasn't more upset. He should be phoning the police, not standing here watching her move about his kitchen as though she owned the place. What was wrong with him? But even as he asked the question, he knew why he wasn't reaching for the telephone. She fascinated him. He'd never met anyone remotely like her before. She'd roused his curiosity to fever pitch. Well, it would be fever pitch if he wasn't so tired. And he couldn't bring himself to believe she was any sort of threat to him. Undoubtedly foolish, but a risk he was willing to take to get to the bottom of the enigma called Mel. He set her mug of steaming chocolate on the island and leaned back against the far counter to sip from his own mug as he watched her work. Wringing her slender neck definitely held some appeal, but he found himself alternately bemused and mesmerized by the small dynamo moving so efficiently about his kitchen as if she'd been doing so for years.

Roderick took pride in the fact that he always maintained control. He was used to being in charge, used to issuing orders and used to being obeyed. His sister often claimed he was part robot. Too bad Pansy couldn't see him trying to deal with this slip of a woman.

"What sort of a name is that for a woman anyhow?"

"Mel? It's short for Melanie," she told him sweetly.

He watched her lift the pan from the burner and flip the egg concoction with a deft flick of her wrist. The eggs rose several inches, turned over and settled back down again as neatly as anything he'd ever seen. Roderick was impressed despite himself.

"Have a seat," she told him.

"I told you I wasn't hungry." But he carried his mug over to the table anyhow.

"Fine, then you can watch me eat your share, too."

Moments later she set half of a fluffy omelet in front of him along with a slice of lightly buttered toast. She settled on the chair across from him with her share.

Roderick Laughlin, wealthy, decisive chairman of the board of several dozen firms, picked up his fork and dutifully cut into the eggs. Cheese oozed from the center. It looked and smelled wonderful, he conceded. It tasted even better. Neither of them spoke until they had cleaned their plates.

"That was excellent," he admitted. "Where did you learn to cook like that?"

"My grandmother taught me. Finish your chocolate while I clean up."

"Leave it. My housekeeper will get the dishes in the morning."

"Absolutely not. I clean up my own messes."

Interesting. And telling, if true.

"Besides, if it keeps snowing like this, your housekeeper isn't going to make it here in the morning. Don't you give your help holidays off? Never mind. You just sit there," she continued, hopping to her feet.

He'd forgotten Sal wouldn't be in tomorrow, which only went to show how tired he was. But Melanie's order to sit caused Roderick to raise an eyebrow in warning. "Has anyone ever told you you're bossy?"

"Yep." She lifted his plate and carried it to the sink.

"Is that why you aren't married?"

Mel whirled, startled. "What?"

Absurdly pleased to have her on the defensive for a change, he watched her turn back to recover the fork she'd dropped into the sink.

"I'm wondering why a woman who can cook like this isn't married."

"Don't ruin your image by telling me you're some backward-thinking male chauvinist," she said, bending to place the fork and the plate in the dishwasher.

"I won't," he promised, waiting to see what she'd do.

She tucked her loose hair back behind her ear and began scrubbing out the pan as he rose and sauntered over to join her at the sink.

"Why would any sane person choose to get married in this day and age?" she demanded.

He watched her scrub the helpless pan faster as her temper rose.

"Marriage is nothing more than a meaningless scrap of paper that everyone ignores until they decide to have it abolished. Then the only happy people are the lawyers."

Rinsing the pan, she slapped it into the dishwasher with noisy force.

"The lawyers make big bucks tearing up the paper right along with people's lives."

She scowled, daring him to contradict her.

"Not fond of lawyers, either, I take it," he taunted her.

"I'd rather be single," she stated belligerently.

"So you prefer to settle for lovers?"

Her glare was meant to intimidate. Since he agreed with her in principle, he was surprised to discover her adamancy disturbed him. He wondered if her parents had been divorced and how old she'd been when it happened or if her own divorce had brought out such strong emotion.

"You're just spoiling for a fight, aren't you? What happened, Roddy, you strike out with the girlfriend tonight?"

He tensed as her barb struck home. "Let's leave Shereen out of this discussion."

"Fine with me. You're the one who brought up the love-life scenario."

She was good at deflecting questions, but he was better. "Who were you running from tonight, Melanie?"

"The big bad wolf."

"After seeing you in that dress, I'm not surprised."

She lifted the whisk she'd used to stir the omelet and aimed it at him as her chin came up defiantly.

"What's wrong with my dress?"

"Well, for one thing, it's missing a lot of material, in case you hadn't noticed."

To his shock, she suddenly giggled then turned away to rinse off the whisk. She had the most amazing giggle.

"Actually I did notice. I nearly froze to death in that dress."

The woman knew how to lead his thoughts astray, but now was not the time to be thinking how sexy she had looked in that tempting bit of green. He forced his mind back to business.

"What were you doing there, Melanie?"

"I prefer Mel and it's none of your business."

"You made it my business when you lifted my wallet and elected to come here tonight."

She turned away and began to wipe off the counters.

"Think what you like."

She shrugged and he watched her generous, unbound breasts rise and fall beneath his shirt. Roderick had no idea what to make of this perplexing woman, but he knew he wanted to know a lot more about her.

"What do you do for a living when you aren't out picking pockets?"

She yawned hugely, rinsed out the cloth she'd been using and draped it neatly over the sink.

"I'm a short-order cook."

He shook his head as she turned around to face him. "If you'd said you were a chef I might believe you after that omelet but…"

"Chefs require fancy degrees these days. Cooks can get jobs anywhere. How's your head?"

He stayed the hand that automatically started toward his temple. The headache that had plagued him all evening was now a negligible throb.

"Better."

He heard the wonder in his voice. She smiled smugly.

"You'll be fine after some sleep. I know I'll feel better. Do you mind if I stay?"

"You are the most extraordinary person."

"Thank you."

Obviously she took that for permission because she turned and preceded him to the stairs. Roderick paused long enough to check that the burner was off, turn out the light and collect his dress shoes before following her up the stairs. At the top, she paused to wish him good-night before heading to the guest room.

She didn't close her door.

Neither did he.

RODERICK WAS ACCUSTOMED to rising early, so it came as a shock when his eyes opened at twenty minutes past nine. More disturbing was the delicious sense of anticipation that filled him.

Melanie was a walking contradiction. Only a professional pickpocket could have removed his keys and wallet as deftly as she'd done. But he would have bet not even a professional thief could have gotten past his security system so effortlessly. She'd also surprised him with her cooking skills. He'd never tasted a better omelet in his life—nor met a woman more enticing. This morning he would have some answers.

He swung his bare legs over the edge of the bed and stood quickly. Nude, he strode into the bathroom and turned on the shower as his mind played back the scenes from last night.

The headache had made him dull. Under normal circumstances he would have forced her to answer his questions then and there. Roderick had few illusions. He was a wealthy man. There were any number of reasons why the woman might have targeted him last night.

Melanie was clever. Her fast staccato speech and apparent twists of dialogue were actually ploys to misdirect a conversation. But the situation still boiled down to the fact that only an accomplished pickpocket could have removed his key case and wallet, and what really stuck in his craw was the ease with which she'd gained access to his home. He and his chief security expert were going to have a few words about that.

Stepping from the shower, he toweled himself vigorously before slathering a thick layer of hot lather over his face. He was anxious to face Melanie again, he realized.

Several minutes later, dressed casually in navy slacks, a white shirt and a navy-and-burgundy sweater that had been a Christmas gift from his sister, Roderick paused to glance inside the open door of the guest room.

The room was empty. There was no sign the room had ever held an occupant. The little minx had even made the bed.

With a muttered curse, he started for the stairs at a run. The aroma of fresh coffee halted him midstride. She hadn't left. Or if she had, he amended, she'd taken time to brew a pot of his favorite blend before leaving. She'd do exactly that, too. The woman did the oddest things. But Roderick found himself descending the stairs at a more reasonable pace.

In the hall outside the kitchen, he hesitated. Melanie's low voice was difficult to hear, but she was speaking with someone.

"I have to go," she said. "He'll be down any minute and I need to be gone…. No, I don't know where I'll stay tonight…. Don't worry, I'll be fine…. Of course I have to do it today. What better chance will I have? With all this snow, no one will be in the building. He won't expect me to hit his office this soon."

Roderick stepped around the corner. Melanie froze in the act of stuffing a wrapped sandwich into the pocket of an old navy peacoat. An apple and four fruit-filled cookies were piled on the counter beside a box of plastic wrap. The silly cow mug his sister had given him was sitting by Melanie's elbow, no doubt holding coffee. She shifted the telephone to her other ear, still listening, but her focus was on him now.

Roderick sent his gaze over the rest of the room. He noted a battered duffel bag leaning drunkenly on the table. A hint of shimmery green material protruded from the opening. Beside it sat a pair of black gloves and a matching hat and heavy wool scarf.

Her expression turned resigned.

"I have to go," she said into the phone without taking her gaze from his. "I didn't make it out soon enough.... No. I'll call you from the hoosegow. You can post my bail. Bye."

He strode over to the island as she replaced the receiver. She was dressed in black, the only exception being her coat—and that dark navy color was close enough. Her unruly mass of hair had been slicked back and confined in an unbecoming ponytail that reached below the top of her sweatshirt.

"I needed five more minutes," she told him calmly.

He leaned against the countertop. "To do what, clean out the silver?"

Blue fire blazed in her eyes.

"Actually, for a wealthy man, you're seriously lacking in small, easily pawnable items of value."

Reaching out, she tore off a bit of plastic wrap and folded it around the cookies.

"But not food, hmm?"

A hint of color darkened her cheeks.

"I like cookies."

She dropped them into the pocket of her coat along with the sandwich.

"So do I," he agreed. "They're more valuable than silver. Silver's hard on the stomach lining. You forgot the apple."

She tore her gaze away and glanced down.

"So I did."

The apple disappeared in the opposite pocket.

"Thanks for reminding me. That should do it."

She took two steps forward and reached for the bag on the table beside him. His hand got there a split second before hers. He felt her shiver when her fingertips touched the back of his hand. She withdrew immediately.

"Now you knew it wasn't going to be this easy, didn't you?" he managed to say lightly.

"It did seem a lot to hope for. You know, if you'd just close your eyes for two minutes, I'd be gone and you could pretend this had all been a dream. I promise, you'll never have to deal with me again."

"Sorry, Melanie, that isn't how this is going to work."

"Mel," she corrected.

The pulse in her neck beat rapidly, denying her outward calm. There was no getting around the fact that Melanie was an appealing waif.

"Why don't you show me what's in the duffel bag?"

Apprehensively, her gaze darted to where it sat on the oval oak table between them.

"I don't have a single thing in there belonging to you, Mr. Laughlin." She inclined her head toward the coffee pot behind her and he followed the gesture to see money sitting on the counter.

"I left you fifty dollars to cover the bed and the sandwich. Sorry if it isn't enough, but it's all I can afford right now."

"I don't want your money, Melanie."

"Mel."

"I want information."

"Try the Internet."

She feinted toward the bag and scooped up her gloves, hat and scarf when his hand closed over the material once more.

"Fine," she told him carelessly, "keep it. I'll never wear that stupid dress again anyhow."

"Pity. I'd like to see you in that dress again. It's perfect for a private party. One where I peel you out of it a tiny bit at a time."

He'd wanted to disconcert her, but the air between them was suddenly rife with a sizzling awareness he hadn't planned on.

"In your dreams, pal."

But her words held the faintest tremor. His lips curved up. That would be a point to him.

"Let's have a look in here, shall we?"

As he opened the duffel bag, her dismay was plain.

"Look, Roddy, you've been very nice up to now. Let's not tarnish your hero image at this point, okay? Let me have that and I'll be on my way."

He removed the shimmering green dress. Beneath it were the matching shoes and a shapeless wool sweater that reminded him of his grandmother. Definitely not something he could picture on Melanie's delicate frame. She backed up several steps and gave a small shrug at his raised eyebrows.

"It's warm."

Roderick turned back to the bag. He found a set of plain underwear and a pair of black sneakers next, but his eyes were riveted on what lay at the bottom of the sack.

The chirp of his security system brought his head up. Melanie was out the back door before he could step around the kitchen table.

Chapter Four

The four inches of new snow on the ground had a solid core of ice beneath, hampering her escape. No wonder there was no traffic. She was guessing the temperature hovered in the teens, making Mel glad she had snagged her hat and gloves before leaving. She'd only pocketed a hundred dollars from her stash this morning, intending to secrete the rest of the bills on her person when she had more time. It was unfortunate that she had overslept.

Maybe if she hadn't taken the time to call her neighbor…but then Claire would have worried. Besides, Mel had needed to know her chances of returning to her apartment. Claire had nixed that immediately. Their building was being watched despite the weather. Mel hoped the watchers were freezing.

She reached the main thoroughfare and crossed the crudely plowed street. Sand and salt crunched beneath her boots. Walking was easier in the road but more dangerous. Mel realized just how dangerous when a green Mercedes pulled alongside her and stopped.

A tiny snowflake landed lightly on her upturned nose as she turned to regard the man behind the wheel. She spared a furious glance at the leaden sky overhead. Thanks to the weather there was nowhere to run. Roderick Laughlin's legs were a lot longer than hers.

"Get in the car, Melanie," he ordered through the open passenger's window.

"I don't think so. It's a lovely day for a walk."

Fluffy white flakes fluttered down from the sky. Roderick opened the driver's door and stepped out. Despite his stormy expression, Mel planted both feet and stood her ground. He strode to the front of the car. Firmly, he opened the passenger door.

"Get...in."

Temptation tested her. She could ignore him and keep walking, but his implacable expression warned her that he'd only come after her. Still, it went against the grain to meekly comply with his order. Mel never had taken well to orders.

"My mother told me never to get in a car with a stranger."

His jaw tightened. "Since we spent the night together, I hardly think I qualify."

She felt the blush riding her cheeks at his mocking tone. "Touché. However, riding with someone when they're angry is a bad idea. You're more apt to have an accident when you're in a temper. Given these road conditions..."

She was prepared for him to come at her. She'd already gauged her chances. She was pretty sure she could make it around the back of the car before he could reach her. If she could get to the driver's door ahead of him, she might be able to slip behind the wheel and leave him standing in the road. She ignored the twinge of conscience that told her it would be a despicable thing to do. What other choice did she have?

"Have it your way then," Roderick said mildly. He

closed the passenger door with barely a sound and started back around the front of the car. "It's a long walk to D.C. from here. I doubt you'll find a cab at any price this morning so enjoy your stroll."

She blinked snowflakes from her lashes. "Wait." The word escaped before she could stop to think. She was poised to run. Thwarted by this unexpected turn, the adrenaline rush had nowhere to go. "You're just going to leave?"

Roderick paused, his hand on the door handle.

"Isn't that what you want?"

"Yes." Of course it was. Wasn't it?

He opened the door.

"No!"

He paused, his expression inscrutable. Snowflakes powdered his dark hair and topcoat. He looked impressively formidable, a powerful force. Her heart thudded painfully against her chest.

"Make up your mind, Melanie."

Walking all the way to D.C. was impossible and she knew it. She'd been acting on impulse since last night. Maybe it was time to start thinking instead.

He hadn't tried to force her into the car. She'd have fought him if he'd attempted it, but he wasn't doing anything predictable. He could have called the police. In his shoes, she certainly would have. But he hadn't and her options were limited and growing more so as the snow began falling in earnest.

"I'll accept your offer."

If he'd looked triumphant or mocking she'd have been tempted to keep walking anyhow, but his expression remained impassive, giving no clue to his thoughts.

"Get in."

What was she doing? This was stupid. Maybe even dangerous. She knew nothing about this man except that he was too rich and too appealing for her peace of mind. So far, his behavior had been that of a complete gentleman. While she wasn't afraid of him, being near him did make her uneasy.

He slid behind the wheel and waited.

It was cold. Mel hated being cold. She opened the passenger door and sank into the thick leather seat, trying not to let him see her shiver. His car was fantastically warm. She wiped the melting snowflakes from her eyes and rubbed her gloved hands together.

Roderick buckled his seat belt, giving hers a meaningful glance. Mel took the hint and snapped hers into place. The back tires spun for a second before finding traction. He eased the car forward over the snow ruts.

"Where are we going?" she asked.

"You tell me."

The anger she'd sensed when he first pulled up beside her was carefully banked, yet his outward calm didn't completely mask his disgruntlement.

"You don't have to take me all the way into D.C.," she told him. "Just drop me at the nearest Metro station."

He shot her an enigmatic look. "You're new to the area, aren't you?"

"No, I've lived here for almost two years now. What does that have to do with anything?"

"If you were a native, you'd know it only takes the threat of snow to paralyze the area. Actual snowflakes cause a complete breakdown. I doubt you'll find the subway or buses running this morning. Only fools or people with no choice are out here right now."

"You don't look like a fool."

He lips curled wryly. "Looks can be deceiving, as you ought to know."

She found herself smiling back and quickly looked away. Good-looking, rich and nice. Sometimes life simply wasn't fair.

They drove in comfortable silence. His gloved hands rested easily on the steering wheel. His profile was strong, compellingly handsome.

"Maybe this isn't such a good idea," she told him. "Just pull over and let me out."

"No."

He didn't even glance at her.

"If it keeps snowing like this, you may have trouble getting back home," she warned.

"Kind of you to be concerned."

"Sarcasm ruins the image, you know."

Surprise whipped his head in her direction for an instant. "Image?"

"Heroes charging to the rescue are not supposed to be sarcastic."

"Is that what you think I'm doing?"

"Isn't it?"

"Hardly."

"Then what are you doing?"

"Damned if I know," he growled under his breath.

She did not want to like him. He could be a most intimidating man when he chose to be. And he was doing that right now. He scowled at the road and the snow peppering their path as if annoyed that it was daring to try and thwart him. A flood of questions lodged in her throat and stuck there until one forced its way past her lips.

"You aren't planning to take me to a police station by any chance are you?"

That brought his head around once more. Meeting those penetrating eyes was more difficult than it should have been. He saw too much. Fortunately, the road conditions demanded his full attention.

"Your belongings are in the back seat," he told her quietly.

She swiveled around. Her scuffed duffel bag looked decidedly out of place against the sumptuous leather. Roderick had seen the contents, yet he hadn't asked a single question. Mel would have given a lot to be able to read his mind right now.

"I might be able to help you," he added softly. "I know a lot of people, Melanie—including some excellent lawyers."

Her breath caught. Having seen the contents he'd made the assumption she would have expected given how they'd met. It shouldn't hurt.

"The name is Mel," she told him coldly. "And if you aren't taking me to the police station, why do you think I need lawyer?"

His eyes left the road again for a second to assess her.

"Talk to me, Melanie."

She shook her head. She had no right to be angry. Of course he thought she was a thief. She hadn't given him any reason to think otherwise. The money resting in the bottom of her duffel bag would only reinforce that belief. Yet he offered his help.

"You know, for a stuffed shirt, you're a pretty nice guy."

"You think I'm a stuffed shirt?"

Mel winced. "Sorry. Sometimes my mouth speaks without permission. Stuffed shirt's a little over the top, but you do come across as rather prim and proper."

His lips nearly formed a smile. "You aren't a friend of my sister's by any chance, are you?"

He had a sister. The knowledge was oddly reassuring. "Not likely. I'm sure we move in different circles."

His jaw set but he ignored the reference to their socio-economic differences.

"You'd like her," he told her calmly. "She thinks I'm a stuffed shirt, too. Maybe I need some new shirts."

"I like your shirts."

Heat swarmed up her neck as they both remembered she'd slept in one.

"The offer to help still stands," he said gently.

Darn. She really didn't want to like him so much. It was so tempting to explain. She only wished she could.

"Thank you," she told him sincerely. "I may need a rain check on that offer if things don't work out."

His lips thinned.

"For now, I'll settle for being dropped off as soon as we cross into D.C. You need to get back before the roads get any worse."

"I'll take you to your front door," he insisted.

She should have known. Stuffed shirts tended to be gentlemen even when they weren't happy.

"Suit yourself, but it won't be the right one."

His gloved hand smacked the steering wheel, startling her.

"Stop playing games, Melanie! You're in trouble. All that money…"

She sucked in a breath. "What about it?"

Mel could almost hear his teeth gnash as he clamped his jaw tightly. He didn't say another word as they crept across the bridge into D.C. Tension hovered between them, an unseen passenger along for the ride.

"Did you count it?" she finally asked to break the silence.

"Of course not!"

She shrugged. "I didn't steal it."

She hadn't meant to add that. It shouldn't matter what he thought.

"You don't trust banks?"

"My parents taught me to keep a stash around for emergencies."

Of course, their idea of an emergency was having enough money to elude the police and disappear at a moment's notice.

"That's quite a stash. You must be facing a serious emergency."

She thought about the dead man in the hotel and shuddered. She'd been blocking that memory ever since she'd found him.

Mel twisted around and reached for her duffel bag. She dug inside and lifted a banded stack of twenties, quickly pulling off several.

Roderick stole a glance in her direction as she folded the money and stuffed it inside her left glove. The rest, she replaced in the bag. Next she removed her tennis shoes. Knotting them together, she hung them around her neck before tossing the duffel bag back on the seat.

"What are you doing?"

"Getting prepared. If you really want to help I'll leave my things here and get them from you later if things work out. If they don't, I'll cash in that rain check."

"Melanie—"

"Mel. Look, you've been great. Don't spoil it with questions I can't answer, okay?"

He pulled the car to the side of the road and stopped. "No, it is not okay. I think I deserve to know what's going on."

"Tough. Go home, Roddy. I appreciate your help. Really."

His eyes narrowed. "What are you into, Melanie?" he enunciated, his voice going dangerously soft.

Unclasping her seat belt, she scooted forward, placed both gloved hands on either side of his face and drew it toward her. His eyes never left hers as she kissed him full on the lips.

Melanie had probably intended for it to be a quick kiss, but Roderick clamped a hand around her neck and held her in place so his lips could move with demand across her own. She started to protest. The moment her lips parted, his tongue invaded her mouth. He made it a bold invasion. A warm, hot quest that tightened his groin and caused her to make a small mew of pleasure deep in her throat.

Roderick's body responded as she plastered herself against him, drawing his tongue inside the hot wet recess of her mouth. He surprised himself with a groan of pleasure as she explored his mouth with a fevered intensity of her own.

When he allowed her to pull back, they were both breathing heavily. Melanie touched her lips with one gloved fingertip.

"Was that what you wanted, Melanie?" he asked, trying to keep his voice level. "A kiss to keep me off balance?"

She scooted away from him across the seat as though scalded. Her hands fumbled for the door handle. He gripped her arm even as she managed to get the door open.

"Don't run. What kind of trouble are you in?"

She struggled. He tightened his hold.

"You said it yourself, Roddy," she spit at him. "I'm a pickpocket and a thief. That's enough trouble for anyone, don't you think?"

He loosened his grip, afraid of hurting her. "You're playing games."

"Hardly."

"Then talk to me!"

"I can't."

His jaw set in frustration. "You mean you won't."

"Yes."

Looking at the determination in those brilliant blue eyes, he knew she wouldn't budge. He could keep her pinned here but it would serve no purpose.

"What would you do if I took you to the nearest police station?"

"Maintain my right to remain silent," she responded promptly.

He let go of her then and she was out of the car before he could change his mind. Roderick watched her scamper down the snow-crusted sidewalk. She rounded the corner onto Twenty-third Street and disappeared from sight. His gaze drifted to the backpack. Was it safe for him to keep that bag? There was still a slim possibility that she was setting him up.

While he hadn't lied about counting the money, the way she had it bundled, he'd guess there were four or five thousand dollars in there. Not a huge sum, but people had died over less.

Who was she?

What was she?

Roderick considered his options. According to the clock on the dashboard, he was supposed to be at the British Ambassador's house in less than an hour. He'd have to call the ambassador to convey his regrets. Fortunately, the weather made a perfect excuse. He doubted many people would be making brunch today.

The Mercedes skidded a bit as he turned it around. He

lifted the car's cell phone and wondered if there was any hope of reaching someone at O'Hearity Investigations today.

MEL CURSED THE SNOW as she studied the apartment building looming before her. Finding a cab had been an incredible bit of luck she hadn't expected. The driver was on his way home and hadn't wanted to take her anywhere at all but he'd stopped when she flagged him down and agreed when she offered to double his fare.

Her gloved hand fingered her lock picks as she stared at the building. They were useless against the computer entry system. A screen and a telephone were recessed into the flat brick wall inside the foyer. A security camera would capture her image the moment she used them.

"Bloody heck."

She touched the scrap of paper in her coat pocket. She'd copied Shereen's address from the leather embossed book she had found on Roderick's nightstand. Fortunately, Shereen wasn't a common name.

Mel wasn't surprised to discover she lived on the top floor of this snobbish, security-conscious condominium. "I should have kept Roderick's keys," she muttered through teeth that were beginning to chatter. No doubt he had access to the building and a key to Shereen's apartment.

Mel eyed the overcast skies. She could stand here and freeze to death or go over there and bluff. Mel tucked her shoes inside her coat, turned up her collar, pulled down her hat, wrapped the scarf around her face and hunkered into her coat to conceal her appearance as much as possible. Crossing the street, she stepped up to the terminal as if she had every right to be there.

Mel found the number for Shereen Oro but deliberately transposed two digits as she typed in the numbers.

"Hello?" The disembodied voice was pure New York Bronx and female.

"Shereen," she said in her best imitation of a southern drawl. "It's Betsy Lynn. Ah'm so sorry to be late, but ah honestly didn't think ah'd get here at all. It's simply beastly outside."

"You've pushed the wrong number," the voice told her.

"Oh," she gasped. "Ah'm terribly sorry to have bothered you."

"Happens all the time. I'll buzz you in."

"Thank you so much. It's terribly kind of you."

At the irritating sound, Mel grabbed the door and darted inside. She didn't have to look around the lobby to know there were cameras fixed on her. The wealthy did have a tendency to trust gadgets for their protection.

When the elevator stopped on the sixth floor, Mel had her lock picks concealed in her hand. Shereen's unit proved to be around the corner from the bank of elevators. The dead bolt on her door was all but worthless and Mel was rewarded with a soft click after only a few seconds.

She stepped inside and nearly cried out as she came face-to-face with her own reflection. The closet doors faced the main entrance and boasted full-length mirrors on both sliding panels. It was enough to give a person a heart attack.

"Ohmygod," she breathed softly. Hopefully, her internal organs would return to their original positions.

And if that wasn't bad enough, somewhere in the apartment water was running. Shereen was home. While Mel expected as much, given the weather, she didn't have a plan for dealing with the model. She'd hoped the woman would still be in bed.

With any luck Mel would find what she needed right

here in the closet. Otherwise she was going to have to leave and wait for Shereen to do the same.

She eased open the far door to find three full-length furs hanging inside.

"Bet the animal rights activists love you," she muttered.

The sable fur she remembered from last night was in front of a silver one. Mel reached for the pocket but her fingers came up empty.

Before she could try the other pocket, the intercom on the wall at her back screamed shrilly. Her heart did another funny slide to the pit of her stomach. She pivoted to glare at the device on the wall. It was too much to hope that there was more than one in the apartment.

Sure enough, the water stopped running. Mel stepped inside the closet and started to close the door. That was when she saw the telltale puddle her boots had left on the richly tiled floor.

Too late.

Hurried footsteps approached. Mel slid shut the door and slipped between the two coats, praying she wouldn't sneeze as the fur tickled her nose. She added another quick prayer that the lofty model wouldn't look down and notice the wet spot on her Tuscan brown floor. And as the footsteps paused on the other side of the door, Mel added a third prayer that whoever was downstairs wasn't planning to come up.

"Shereen? Larry Wilhelm."

"You made excellent time."

Shereen had one of those deep, throaty voices that sounded patently phony to Mel, but then she wasn't a hormone-driven male.

"I walked over. It seemed safer than driving given the road conditions, but it's a good thing your apartment is only a few blocks from mine. It's freezing out here."

"Well come on up. I can promise you it's not freezing in here."

She made it sound like an invitation to bed. Heck, maybe it was. Mel didn't care. Wilhelm would have a coat—a wet, snow-covered coat. A coat that hopefully the fastidious Shereen would not want to hang inside this closet. Otherwise Mel would need Roderick's lawyer after all.

Footsteps hurried away. Mel reached into the coat's other pocket. She experienced a moment of panic when it also felt empty at first, but her fingers located Boswell's key case at the bottom along with the slim plastic card she had taken from the dead man. She transferred both to her own pocket, ignoring the way her nerves were lunching on her stomach lining.

Before she could leave she heard Shereen returning. As silently as possible, Mel moved farther back until she was tucked between the silver fur and a thick black fur at the far end of the closet. There wasn't much space, but as long as Shereen opened the other side of the closet she might not notice her uninvited guest.

A heavy hand rapped solidly against the front door. Mel held her breath.

"Larry," Shereen cooed a minute later. "Do come in. You look positively frozen."

"I am. You, on the other hand, look absolutely breath-taking."

"Thank you," she purred. "Let me get your coat."

Mel closed her eyes and tried to shrink, praying for a miracle. She got one as the closet door slid back on the side farthest from her. Opening her eyes she saw a slim hand reach inside. Long red talons lifted an empty hanger and disappeared from view.

"Goodness, your coat is sopping wet. It must be snowing harder than I realized."

"It's coming down pretty good out there. They're calling for several more inches before the day is over. It's a major storm. Even worse, the temperature is dropping. The whole mess is expected to freeze tonight."

"That will certainly make tomorrow's rush hour fun."

The nails reappeared. Coats were shoved back, practically suffocating Mel as a man's wet topcoat was suspended in front to give it plenty of space to drip without touching anything else.

"I doubt anyone will be going anywhere come morning," the man called Larry was saying. "And I seem to have created quite a puddle on your floor."

Good. Then no one would notice the one Mel had already made there.

"That's why I pay a cleaning service. Now slip out of those wet boots and come inside by the fire."

"These apartments have fireplaces?"

"Yes, wonderful gas ones. You just flip a switch. They make everything so cozy on a miserable day like this, don't you think?"

"Where's Laughlin? I thought he'd be here, as well, after he heard what happened last night."

Mel tensed. There was a ladylike snort as a boot landed against the marble floor on the other side of her hiding spot.

"I'm afraid Mr. Laughlin and I came to a parting of the ways last night."

"Oh? I'm sorry to hear that."

"Are you?" the voice asked archly. "I'm not. Roderick and I didn't have all that much in common as it turns out."

"Lovers' quarrel?"

A second boot joined the first.

"No, Roderick doesn't quarrel. He prefers to give ultimatums. I realize a man in his position is used to giving orders and having them obeyed, but I'm not one of his employees. I don't take well to ultimatums."

"I can imagine."

Amusement laced his voice, but Mel detected a note of speculation, as well. She wondered if the man was starting to feel more like a victim than a guest.

"Let's move into the living room," Shereen invited. "Would you care for a drink?"

"No, thanks. You said you had something you wanted to discuss. I'll just have some coffee if you have any made."

"Freshly brewed. I have a special blend ground just for me at that delightful little bistro down the street."

"I know the place you mean. They have some great pastries as well as good coffee."

"And I just happen to have some of their pastries to go with our coffee."

As the voices moved farther away, Mel quickly slid open the panel and nearly fell over a pair of expensive boots forming a massive puddle in the small foyer.

"Excuse me a minute, Shereen. I need to get my cell phone from my coat pocket. I'm expecting a call that I really have to take."

Mel opened the front door and scooted into the hall, nearly ramming into the man standing there with his fist raised to knock.

He made a startled sound of surprise, but there was no time to wonder what Roderick was doing here. Mel shoved him back and twisted around—too late to catch the door to keep it from making noise as it closed. While it didn't slam, there was no way the people inside could have missed the sound. Mel grabbed Roderick's coat sleeve and tugged. She'd have had more luck with a sack of concrete.

"Move!" she hissed. "I'll explain later."

Without pausing to see if he followed, Mel sprinted down the hall.

Chapter Five

"What do you think you are doing?" Roderick demanded harshly, gripping Melanie's coat and forcing her to a halt just short of the elevators.

"Trying to escape. Come with me and I'll explain!" Somehow.

"Explain now. What were you doing inside Shereen's apartment?"

"We don't have time for this!"

Mel jerked free and pressed the down button. Thankfully no one had called for the elevator since Roderick had used it. The doors opened instantly. She darted inside and pressed the lobby button. Right before the doors slid shut, Roderick filled the remaining space.

If her system hadn't already been on an adrenaline overload, his grim expression would have put it there. The close confines made him loom even larger than she knew him to be. He was all male and he was very angry.

"Okay, look, I left something in your date's coat pocket last night." She whipped out the black leather key case. "I dropped this in Shereen's pocket when we were going down the escalator."

His expression shouted his disbelief.

"Do you always carry a man's key case?"

She would have preferred him to yell at her. That icy, dead tone was far more daunting than a raised voice would have been.

"Absolutely. Men's key cases are the newest fashion trend."

His scowl deepened. Her chest felt as if it would explode.

"I would have gotten it for you if you had asked."

"Oh, I couldn't do that. I mean, the two of you are on the outs. I didn't want you to have to call her on my account."

"What makes you think we're on the outs?"

Bloody heck. Should she tell him his model was upstairs with his replacement?

"You mean besides the fact that you came home alone last night? Hey, it's none of my business. I just figured it would be quicker if I retrieved the keys myself."

"By breaking into Shereen's apartment."

"I didn't exactly break in, I sort of…let myself in."

"Without permission."

"Well, yes, but only because I didn't want to have to make a bunch of excuses. And I only went as far as the hall closet in the foyer. Honest."

Stone was more expressive than his features.

"Give me one good reason why I should believe a thing you say, Melanie."

"That's an easy one. I'm a lousy liar. No, really. I am. Okay, I know the situation looks bad on the surface, but I can explain everything."

"Of course you can. For someone who doesn't lie, you have an exceptionally glib tongue."

She tried for humor. "What can I say? It's a gift."

His expression didn't soften.

"Save it until we reach the car. Then I expect you to tell me what's really going on—including how you knew where to find Shereen. And I'm warning you, Melanie, if I don't like your explanations you're going to have a chance to use that glib tongue to talk your way out of jail."

She flinched. "I think you mean that."

"I do."

"Bloody heck."

"Where did you pick up that expression?"

She shrugged. "I read a lot."

The elevator came to a smooth stop. As the doors began to part, Roderick's hand clamped down on her arm once more.

"The garage is on the next level down. And don't even think of trying to run off."

He pressed the button and the doors closed once more. A quick glance at the set of his jaw convinced Mel this was no time to argue. And why argue? He had a car. A car would get her to her next destination much quicker than walking. She wasn't likely to luck into another taxi ride today no matter how much money she offered to pay.

"You can let me go now. I'm more anxious than you are to get out of here."

"Why?"

She nodded at the camera cleverly concealed above them. "Buildings with security cameras make me nervous. I don't like unseen eyes watching me."

"Then you won't enjoy a jail cell."

The elevator stopped and the doors opened. Her shiver could have been from his words or the bitingly cold wind that whistled through the underground garage. The arctic air didn't seem to bother Roderick. She had to practically run to keep up with his long stride. Their footsteps echoed eerily in the cavernous space. Mel peered around nervously. Parking garages always made her edgy, not that any self-respecting mugger would be out on a day like this. Still, she was glad when the familiar green Mercedes finally came into view.

"You couldn't find a parking space any farther away?"

Roderick's only response was to hold the passenger door open for her. He waited for her to get settled before he shut the door firmly. The simple act of courtesy further unsettled her. Mel knew he was furious, but he was so self-contained it was scary. Once seated, however, he showed no inclination to start the engine.

"Let's go," she urged.

He reached over and pulled her scarf down to reveal her features.

"Who do the keys belong to Melanie?"

Her heart sank. She'd known this escape had been too easy.

"I can't tell you."

His jaw clenched. He started the key toward the ignition.

"Wait!"

"You stole the keys from someone."

"You could say that, yes."

"Why?"

"Because using a key is easier than picking a lock and I need them to find something." That wasn't going to satisfy him. She'd already figured out that Roderick Laughlin was tenacious.

"What do you have to find, Melanie?"

There was only one thing to do. "My sister is being blackmailed," she lied. "The evidence is in an office building. If I can get to it before her lover realizes my goal, she'll be off the hook and I can save her marriage. Now will you take me to M Street or not?"

It was hard to meet his intent gaze. She had to force herself not to look away. He pushed the key into the ignition and gave it a turn. Unlike her car, his engine purred to life.

"You're right, Melanie. You don't lie worth a damn."

She sighed heavily. "I told you so. You may as well drive me to the police station. I can't tell you what I'm looking for."

"Because of your sister."

"I don't have a sister," she admitted.

"I didn't think so. What else did you take?"

"Nothing! I told you, I didn't go any farther than the hall closet. I wanted the keys so I looked up her address in the book on your nightstand."

He took that without comment. "And if I hadn't come along, what were you going to do next?"

Mel squirmed. "You don't want to know."

"Yes. I do."

The exasperating man wasn't going to budge. She couldn't think of any more half truths to tell him so she offered him a fierce look and sank back against the cushy seat.

"I'm going to break into an office building."

It gave her a small sense of satisfaction to watch shock overtake his grim expression.

"You mean that!"

"Of course I do. You said you wanted to help me so help me. I need a ride to M Street. Will you take me there?"

"No!"

She reached for the door handle. He was quicker.

"You aren't going anywhere, Melanie."

"Not if you don't let go of my wrist, but sooner or later someone from security is going to want to know why we're sitting here like this. Do you really want to answer their questions? I don't. If you won't take me to M Street let's at least get away from here because unless your girlfriend and her guest suddenly went deaf, they must have heard her front door close."

"What guest?"

Oops.

"I didn't wait around for an introduction." She wanted to leave it there, but she owed him. "Look, if Shereen is important to you then you ought to go back upstairs and talk to her," she said earnestly.

Roderick was quick. Immediate understanding showed in his dark eyes but he didn't release her arm.

"Shereen is not important at the moment. I can get my key back later. You're the one I want to talk with."

"Thanks, but I don't consider that an honor and I really don't have time for a heart-to-heart chat right now."

"Make time. How do you plan to get inside this office building? It's New Year's Day in case you've forgotten."

Mel squirmed. "That's what the keys are for."

"You use cards, not keys to access buildings these days—as I'm sure you know quite well. What else was in that coat pocket, Melanie?"

"Has anyone ever told you that you can be a pain in the butt?"

"Frequently."

She wanted to smile at his deadpan delivery. "I promise I'm not out to hurt anyone or cause trouble. My methods may be a bit unorthodox—"

"A bit?"

"It's what I do."

"You're a professional thief?"

"Of course not. I told you, I'm a short-order cook." She held his gaze and tried to convey all the sincerity in her heart. "Please. This is important. If I could tell you what's going on I would. I figure I owe you that much, but I can't and I won't."

Over his shoulder she spotted movement. A vehicle was heading slowly in their direction. "I'd make up my mind if I were you," she told Roderick. "I think someone finally woke up in the security office."

Roderick released her and followed her gaze. He put the car into Reverse and backed up.

"I hope you don't mind if I look like I'm yelling at you," she told him. "If they think we're having a fight they probably won't stop us. It would help if you could manage to look angry."

"That won't be difficult," he muttered.

The uniformed man in the SUV looked them over closely as the two cars passed. He didn't stop them, and even looked a bit sympathetic as Melanie continued mouthing words and gesturing angrily. Still, Roderick had no doubt he'd check out the license plate to be sure the car was authorized to be in this parking garage. He doubted Shereen had thought to notify them otherwise.

They weren't stopped at the control booth, though Roderick almost wished they had been. Snow blanketed the street, reducing visibility to almost zero. An intelligent person would stay put until things improved. Funny, he used to consider himself quite intelligent. Common sense seemed to go straight out the window around Melanie and he couldn't for the life of him figure out why. She was doing all she could to get rid of him. So why didn't he walk away?

Because she intrigued him. And if nothing else, Roderick felt compelled to discover what she was up to.

Going to Shereen's apartment had been a spur-of-the-moment decision on his part. He'd planned to ask for his house key back before returning to Virginia. The last thing he'd expected was to find his secretive Cinderella looking like a bank robber as she pelted out Shereen's front door.

Cinderella. Weird how that stupid story kept popping into his head. The only thing princely about him was his portfolio and Melanie didn't seem interested. It rankled that she seemed so bent on getting rid of him.

The car slewed as it found a particularly treacherous spot under the snow.

"The roads are getting worse, aren't they?" she asked.

"Yes. What address do you want?"

"There's a parking garage up ahead. You can pull in there."

"Is this the building you want or are you planning to give me the slip again?"

Her expression told him it was the latter.

"Save us both some grief. Tell me where you're going. I'll drop you off and wait for you."

Nice to see he could at least rattle her. Those incredibly soft lips parted in surprise, but she quickly recovered.

"Why would you do that?"

Good question. "Call it extreme curiosity. You do know what you're doing, don't you?"

"Of course."

She really was a bad liar.

She sighed heavily. "Okay. It's the next building over. The one with the flag on top."

In the swirling snow he could barely make out the next building over, let alone a flag on top, but he certainly knew which building she meant. His heart tripped a little faster. He'd been curious before, now he knew he'd do whatever it took to find out what she was up to. Despite the driving conditions, he risked another look at her.

Melanie perched on the edge of her seat. She peered straight ahead, chewing on her lower lip distractedly. Instead of stopping out front he turned down the side street.

"What are you doing?"

He turned into the mouth of a chained parking lot at the rear of the building.

"Now what?" he asked, putting the car in Park.

She offered him a saucy grin and pulled the scarf back up to cover her features.

"Now, you wait like you said you would. I shouldn't be more than fifteen or twenty minutes, tops."

Her gloved hand reached out and squeezed his arm before she opened the passenger door, letting in a blast of arctic air and snow. With a jaunty thumbs-up she hurried down the sidewalk toward the rear entrance.

Roderick gave her four minutes before he stepped from the car and unlocked the chain. Although tempted to leave the Mercedes where it was, he was afraid security would think it had broken down and go looking for him.

He pulled the car into the lot, turned it around and replaced the chain. Melanie had better not be able to get inside. His sister kept telling him the building needed better security. If Melanie did get in he'd never hear the end of it.

Her footprints were rapidly filling with snow as he followed the disappearing tracks. So she did have a key card as well as keys. Who had she taken them from?

The trail ended at the glass-enclosed entrance. Roderick entered the lobby and realized there were no wet prints on the richly marbled floor. He puzzled over that for a second until he remembered her tennis shoes. The little imp must have changed out of her boots in the entranceway so as not to leave a trail inside.

The guard station was vacant. Luck or planning on her part? Probably, Pete was making his rounds or using the bathroom—unless he was chasing Melanie. Roderick worried about that thought for less than a second. The building was almost eerily silent. A chase would involve noise.

Frankly, Roderick was surprised Pete wasn't watching the Rose Bowl on a portable TV. Though new, Pete was a conscientious employee but an avid football fan and there was no reason for him to be expecting trouble on a day like this.

Roderick strode to the desk and signed in before heading to the elevator.

"Oh, Mr. Laughlin. It's you, sir," Pete said, hurrying around the corner near the bathrooms. "Happy New Year, sir. I was down the hall when I heard you come in. What on earth are you doing out on a day like this?"

An excellent question.

"Happy New Year, Pete. I need some paperwork from my office but I'll be leaving shortly."

"On New Year's Day, sir?" The man cocked his head and frowned.

"You're working, aren't you?" Roderick pointed out.

"Only because I have three kids and you pay time-and-a-half on holidays," the man said with an engaging smile. "Besides, my in-laws are staying over. This is the only peace and quiet I've had since Christmas."

Roderick's lips lifted in a brief smile as he stepped inside the waiting elevator and let it carry him to the top floor. Anger quickly replaced his good humor. The blasted woman was forcing him into an untenable situation. Calling the police was the last thing he wanted to do until he knew what was going on, but it appeared she was going to leave him no choice. What the devil was she up to?

The hall on the top floor stretched dark and empty. The reception area appeared undisturbed but he wasn't surprised. Melanie would have taken the stairs rather than alert Pete by using the elevator. She'd be here any second, so he leaned back against the glass wall and planned what he'd say when she arrived.

Only she didn't. When his Rolex told him that more than five minutes had passed, he knew he'd been suckered by his own arrogance. She wasn't coming—at least not to this floor. He'd made the assumption because of the way she'd singled him out at the party, at his home, breaking into Shereen's apartment then coming here to his building. It had seemed likely that her next step would be his office. He should have known better. Melanie never did the expected.

His company only used the top four floors. The rest of the building was leased to other tenants. He knew them all, of course, but he'd have to concentrate to remember who occupied which floor. He debated his options and headed for the stairwell. Melanie could be anywhere by now.

His irritation mounted in direct proportion to his concern. Melanie claimed she wasn't a thief, yet her actions said otherwise. His desire to protect her had been as ridiculous as it was out of character. He should have reported her the moment he discovered she'd picked his pocket.

He nearly slid on a small puddle on the fourth floor stairwell. A pair of simple black boots sat in the corner near the door. The melting snow was seeking a low spot, leaving a trail. She hadn't thought of everything.

Aggravation melded with banked anger and a growing curiosity. This floor housed his research and development group. His thoughts immediately turned to Larry Wilhelm. He didn't want Melanie to turn out to be a spy for Wilhelm or one of his other competitors, but what else could she be doing here?

Roderick stepped into the empty corridor. It was too much to hope she'd be standing around in plain sight. He strode down the hall, giving his anger free reign. The lady was obviously a professional thief despite her protestations.

A muffled noise brought his head around.

If he hadn't come to a stop in the silent hall opposite Carl Boswell's office he wouldn't have heard the small thump at all. A sinking sensation started in the pit of his stomach. Melanie was in Carl's office?

Carl was more than his vice president in charge of research and development. The man and his wife had been good friends of his for years. The sinking sensation swelled as he thought back to his conversation with a slightly inebriated Joyce Boswell at the office Christmas party. Morosely she had confided that she thought Carl was involved in an affair.

Roderick hadn't known what to say. Carl and Joyce had been married more than fifteen years. He'd thought they were perfectly suited. Carl was always talking about his family—until recently. He'd been acting strangely. Several things had bothered Roderick over the past few weeks, including the way Carl had been avoiding him. He should have confronted his friend instead of waiting until the holidays were over.

Was it even remotely possible that Melanie's fabrication had held an element of truth earlier? What if she was there to recover a personal item?

Melanie and Carl?

The idea sent a spike of rare fury down his spine. Roderick didn't want to think about an alliance between them, much less believe they were lovers. He reached for the doorknob. Surprisingly, it twisted beneath his fingers.

Careless of her. Melanie should have relocked the door. He entered the administrative assistant's office and peered around. The room was neat and orderly as always. Whatever sound had caught his attention initially, there was no noise now. Quietly, he moved around the desk and headed for the private office on the right.

Melanie whirled when he opened the inner door. The small safe concealed in the cherry file cabinet yawned open. Her gloved hands held a sheaf of papers. She'd been going through them quickly. He noted other items in neat piles on the wide cherry desktop. The scarf still covered her face, but there was raw fear in her china-blue eyes.

Cold rage washed over him. No matter why she was here, this wasn't an action he could brush aside. A pickpocket was one thing. Going through a company safe was something else altogether.

Roderick leashed his anger and leaned against the doorjamb. "I warned you that you wouldn't like going to jail," he said conversationally.

"Ohmygod, you scared me to death," she accused. "What are you doing in here? You promised to wait in the car."

She had the audacity to sound outraged. He eyed her with his most steely expression. "I said I'd wait. I never said where."

"How did you—? Never mind. Did you touch anything besides the door handle?"

This was not the reaction he'd expected. "What?"

"Keep your voice down! There's a watchman in the building."

"I know."

Melanie shuffled through the papers quickly, scanning some, stopping to read others more closely. Roderick blinked back surprise. He couldn't believe she was calmly going through his vice president's papers with him standing right there. Was it possible she didn't know who he was?

He came away from the door and crossed the plush white carpet in three long strides. She didn't bother to look up. She had come to a large manila envelope that she fingered then opened.

"What do you think you are you doing?" he demanded harshly.

Somehow, the act of opening that envelope seemed more outrageous than anything else she had done so far.

A key fell out and bounced to the top of the desk. She snatched for it before it could fall to the floor. Roderick glimpsed a DVD case and several papers before she resealed the envelope and slid it inside the open front of her coat. She zipped it closed. The key disappeared into a coat pocket.

"Don't touch the desk," she warned.

Incredulous, Roderick watched as she scooped up the rest of the papers and began putting them back in the safe. That was when he saw the stack of currency sitting inside. His gut twisted.

What was Carl doing with a wad of cash in his office safe?

Melanie pulled the money out to work a thick file back in place. She repositioned the bills without interest, although the top denomination was a hundred dollars. She relocked the safe with the quick, economical movements of a pro.

If the quiet hadn't been so hushed, he would have missed the faint whir of the elevator starting up. The office backed to one of the shafts, he remembered.

"Bloody heck. We have to go, now!"

For such a petite woman, she could move like a human dynamo.

"What did you touch?" she asked imperatively. "Hurry!"

Roderick debated only a second. "The doorknobs."

"Okay. Walk straight to the hall and don't touch another thing."

Roderick followed her into the outer office and watched as she relocked the inner office door and wiped the doorknob with a man's navy-colored handkerchief.

"Let's go," she whispered urgently.

In the hall, the sound of the rising elevator was clear. He'd never realized how much noise they made when the building was empty like this. Melanie closed and locked the outer door and wiped that handle, as well.

"Run!"

She sprinted for the stairwell at the far end of the hall. Roderick followed on her heels. They plunged through the doorway. Melanie turned to shove at the heavy steel in an effort to force the door closed more quickly. The elevator ground to a halt. She muttered what sounded like a low oath. Scooping up her boots, she started to go down the stairs. Roderick caught her arm before she had taken more than a step.

"This way," he insisted. Holding her firmly, he half tugged her up the next flight of stairs.

"We'll get trapped up here!"

"Trust me," he ordered.

"Bloody heck."

But she followed, passing him once he let go of her arm. When she would have turned into the corridor of the next floor he merely shook his head and pointed up. Her eyes were mutinous but she didn't waste time arguing. She would have continued up to the roof if he hadn't grabbed her arm to indicate the top floor. In the hall she whirled to face him.

"Are you out of your mind? Now we'll be trapped up here!"

Instead of answering, Roderick pulled the key card from his pocket. Disgusted for feeling winded when she wasn't even breathing hard, he spared a thought to wonder how long it had been since he'd gone downstairs to use the gym.

New Year's resolution number two. Twice a week from now on no matter how busy he was, he'd make time for the gym.

Resolution number one—avoid kooky pickpockets.

Her eyes widened as he unlocked the main door. She looked from the brass nameplate to his face. Amazing how much he could read in the flick of her eyes.

"Your office," she said flatly.

"My building," he stated.

Chapter Six

"Bloody heck."

"Succinctly put," Roderick agreed. He led the way back to his private sanctum and unlocked the door. For the first time in twenty-four hours, he felt in control.

"There's a washroom through there." He pointed at the closed door. "When Pete comes in, just step inside."

"Pete?"

"The security guard from downstairs."

She muttered something under her breath.

"What was that?"

"What makes you think he'll come here?"

She whipped off her scarf and glared at him.

"For one thing, he knows I'm in the building. He'll stop by when he makes his rounds. For another, he isn't going to miss the puddle your wet boots left in the stairwell. Pete is extremely conscientious."

A flare of what might have been panic came and went in her eyes.

"We can't stay here!"

"Yes we can. Set those wet boots in the sink in the bathroom."

For a moment, he thought she was going to turn and

leave, but scowling she did as he directed. Returning to the office, she stalked to the large picture window behind his desk and stared fiercely out at the falling snow.

"Unless your vision is better than mine there isn't much to see out there."

She turned back to him, upping her glare another notch.

Roderick unlocked his desk and drew out a sheaf of papers. He spread them across his desktop in an array that looked busy.

"What are you doing?" she demanded.

"Setting the stage. I told Pete I was coming up here to collect some work."

"On New Year's Day?"

"That's what he said."

Shedding his coat, Roderick draped it over a chair before crossing the room to the bar. From the tiny refrigerator, he added ice to a tall glass and filled it three-quarters full from a can of soda.

"I'd offer you a drink, but a second glass would cause explanations I don't think either of us want to make right now. However, feel free to drink from the can if you're thirsty." He set both on the desk, turned on the reading lamp, picked up a pen and sank into the soft leather chair behind the desk.

"You're a workaholic."

"Are you sure you don't know my sister?"

She muttered something under her breath.

"I didn't catch that."

"How many security people do you have inside the building?"

He forced his tone to remain light though his jaw tightened. "Forget it, Melanie. We're going to talk."

"I'm not feeling real chatty right now."

"Too bad. Tell me about your relationship with Carl Boswell."

She jerked as if he'd struck her.

"He works for you!"

"Vice president in charge of research and development," he agreed. "How long have you and Carl been lovers?"

"What?"

"Secrets rarely stay that way," he chided. The tight, raw anger at the thought of the two of them together continued to surprise him. "You do know he already has a wife and three children, don't you? He's very fond of them. *All* of them. So am I," he added in warning.

"Why would you think…? Because I told you that stupid story about my nonexistent sister?"

"And you have his keys and his security card to the building," he added.

"What a mess."

She began to pace, short choppy steps to and fro before his desk. He watched intently, trying to puzzle out her thoughts. Her reaction wasn't what he'd expected, but that should have been a given. Melanie never did the expected.

"You aren't his type, you know."

And she wasn't. Carl had never been a womanizer, nor was he the sort to turn a woman's head. A plain-looking man with oversized ears and frown lines etched on his forehead, Carl had started to develop a slight paunch to go with his receding hairline. Roderick would have said there wasn't an adventurous bone in his friend's middle-aged body.

"And you would know, I suppose," she replied sarcastically.

It was hard to picture his dependable, plodding friend initiating an affair. Carl and Melanie together made no sense. For one thing, Melanie wouldn't know how to plod if someone gave her directions. Maybe that's what had attracted Carl.

Melanie wasn't exactly the sort to turn a man's head, either—except dressed in that flashy green number she'd worn when they met. Okay, she was attractive in her own way, but nothing like Shereen.

"So what was the draw?" he asked, truly curious. She gave him a flat look that told him exactly what he could do with his curiosity.

Roderick leaned back without taking his eyes from her. "How did you meet Carl? He's so involved in his work and family that he rarely has time to go anywhere these days. Of course, he does love opera and the ballet," Roderick mused. "But you don't strike me as the classical type."

She stopped pacing. "Bloody heck."

"Yes, well, I'm not an opera fan myself."

"This is turning into a farce."

"I had noticed."

Placing small neat hands flat on his desk, she leaned down, holding his gaze.

"I am not Carl's lover," she enunciated clearly. Crystal-blue eyes shimmered with intensity. "I have never been his lover. I never even met the man."

Roderick found himself wanting to believe her. "So you stole his keys and security card for the sole purpose of coming here to steal…what?"

Mutely, Melanie sank down into one of the cream-colored visitor's chairs across from him. Fluctuating expressions crossed her pinched features.

"Are you going to deny the charge?" he prodded.

"Is there any point?"

"So you did pick his pocket."

"In a manner of speaking."

She would no longer meet his eyes. Roderick was almost as startled as she was when his fist came down on the desktop, scattering papers and sloshing soda across the desk.

"Stop playing games! I want answers!"

A responding spark of anger sent her leaning forward once more. "Listen, bucko—"

But they both heard the outer office door opening. Roderick gestured toward the bathroom. Melanie was already on her feet, darting inside.

"Mr. Laughlin?"

Roderick grabbed a fistful of tissues and began mopping at the spilled drink. "In my office. Come on back, Pete."

Pete stepped inside, his alert gaze sweeping the room. "Sorry to barge in on you like this, sir, but we may have an intruder in the building."

Tossing the wet tissues in the wastebasket, Roderick looked up and waited.

"None of the alarms have gone off, but I came across a puddle in the stairwell on four. There are damp spots on the carpeting leading to Mr. Boswell's office, sir."

Roderick forced himself to appear relaxed. "My fault, Pete. I took the steps down there right after I came up here. I thought I needed to pull some papers from his office until I remembered I had the information in some other files." He indicated the papers spread across his desk.

"Yes, sir. My first thought was that might be the case. And that would explain the damp carpeting all right, but unless you stood on the landing for several minutes, it doesn't explain the puddle, sir."

Roderick cursed his stupidity and wondered how he'd

let himself get into this situation in the first place. He was
sorely tempted to open the bathroom door and turn Melanie over to Pete and the police. Knowing that he wasn't
going to do exactly that only added to his irritation.

"A leak maybe?"

"No, sir."

He forced his fingers to remain unclenched. "Have you
called the police?"

"No, sir. Since none of the alarms went off, I called my
supervisor. He's sending a team to help me sweep the
building, but in this weather…" He shrugged, indicating
help probably wouldn't arrive immediately.

Roderick nodded at the reprieve. "I assume nothing appears to have been tampered with?" If Melanie had left
other traces it was best to know now.

"Not that I saw, sir."

"If there had been anything to see, you'd have noticed,
Pete. The police department lost a fine officer when you
had to retire on disability."

"Thank you, sir. To be safe, you should keep your doors
locked until I'm sure the building is secure."

"I don't expect to be here much longer."

"If you wouldn't mind, buzz me when you're ready to
leave, sir."

"All right."

He followed Pete back through the main office, lock-
ing the door behind the guard. Melanie waited in front of
his desk, her damp boots clutched in one hand.

"Great," she greeted him. "Do you see what you've done?"

"Saved your neck?"

"If you'd waited in the car like you promised my neck
wouldn't have needed saving! I would have been in and
out of here in fifteen minutes, tops."

Roderick stared in disbelief. "Pete still would have found the puddle from your boots."

"So what?" She aimed a finger at his chest as her irritation grew. "I'd have been gone and he'd have simply had a mystery on his hands. But no, you had to go and tramp all over the hall in wet boots."

"I don't believe this."

"Me, either. Now how are we going to get out of here?" She began to pace again.

"You ought to give that man a raise, you know. Not many rent-a-cops would have even noticed the water. I mean, who checks stairwells in an empty building?"

Roderick fought an urge to reach out and shake the infuriating woman. "You know, you're coming perilously close to bringing out a violent streak I never suspected was part of my nature. Sit down."

"Are you crazy?"

"No, but I'm getting there. Sit…down!"

He was slightly surprised when, after a moment's hesitation, she obeyed.

"Give me those blasted boots." He strode to the bathroom and set them back in the sink. When he returned, Melanie had withdrawn a slightly mashed sandwich from her pocket along with the apple and the cookies.

"Do you have any ginger ale?" she asked.

"You're going to eat that now?"

"Unless I'm free to go."

He shook his head to keep from shaking her. She unwrapped the sandwich with slow deliberation. Roderick watched her sink small white teeth into the dark pumpernickel bread. She chewed thoroughly before swallowing.

"You want the other half?" she offered.

His own teeth actually gnashed.

"They'll probably do an office-by-office search, you know," she told him. "And this plush little sanctuary won't be exempt." She bit off another bite.

Throttling her was becoming more and more appealing. Only her tight grip on the defenseless bread assured him that her casual manner was an act.

"What makes you think I won't turn you over to them when the others get here?" he asked.

She shrugged and carefully rewrapped the sandwich. Roderick walked to within inches of her chair. When she shrugged again, he gripped her arms and drew her to her feet.

Vivid blue eyes widened in shock. The sandwich fell to the floor.

"You aren't cute and you aren't beautiful, but you certainly do know how to climb under a man's skin."

"Let go of me!"

Her hair, in its tight ponytail, was tangled from her hat. Several wisps had broken free to drift against her cheeks. Creamy and smooth, only the scar on her forehead marred the perfection of her skin. She was startled rather than frightened, but he was pleased to see she was no longer so sure of herself. It was about time to turn the tables. Lightly, he allowed his finger to trace the scar.

"Where did you get this?"

Wariness replaced her startled expression. A flash of awareness told him she was suddenly seeing him as a man and not merely a sparring partner. The tip of her tongue darted out to moisten delicate pink lips. Erotically tempting, but not a deliberate ploy he decided, more of a nervous reaction.

Still, he had a crazy urge to taste those lips again. He could see why Carl might have risked an affair with her.

There was something oddly tempting about Melanie. Roderick suspected it was that she was so intensely alive. She reminded him of a hummingbird. So much energy. If she turned that intensity on a man…well, she certainly would not be a passive lover.

She made one more halfhearted effort to pull free and glowered at him.

"If you must know, I fell off a roof and landed on a rock when I was a kid."

"Of course you did." He could picture the scene clearly. Brown hair flying, scabbed-over knees—because she would have been an intrepid little girl—she probably had all the neighborhood boys jumping all sorts of hoops to keep up with her. He doubted there was much she wouldn't dare.

"Satisfied?" she demanded.

He almost smiled. "Not by a long shot," he told her softly.

Her cheeks pinked at his provocative tone. With a belligerent bravado he was certain she no longer felt, she demanded, "Where did you get yours?"

His humor faded at the stark memory. "A bar fight," he told her flatly.

"You're kidding. It's hard to picture you in a bar much less a brawl. You aren't the type to throw the first punch and I can't imagine anyone strong enough to ignore one of your intimidating glares."

"You don't seem to be having much of a problem."

"I've got an older brother." Her eyes darkened. "Besides, I don't have time to be intimidated."

"Why not?"

Her lips pursed. The pulse point in her neck beat rapidly. He had the most outrageous vision of bending to taste that spot.

"Look, as much as I'd enjoy standing here sparring with you all day, this is getting us nowhere," she huffed.

"I noticed."

There had been the slightest quaver in her voice. Melanie wasn't nearly as smug as she wanted him to believe.

"On the other hand," he added, "you should know that I've always enjoyed a challenge."

Before he could change his mind he reached out and grasped both her wrists in one hand, holding them over her head.

Melanie tried to pull free. "What are you doing?"

He tightened his grip.

"Let go of me!"

"In a minute." With his other hand, Roderick drew down the zipper of her coat.

"Stop that!"

She tried to jerk away but he moved in close so she had no space to maneuver. He removed the packet she'd taken from Carl's safe and tucked inside her jacket. Tossing it on the desk, he ran his hand as impersonally as possible over her trim body. She promptly kicked him in the shin.

"That hurt," he told her mildly.

"Let go of me!"

Twisting, she attempted to break his grip.

"Hold still," he commanded. His hand brushed across her breast. Instantly, she went motionless. So did he. The very air around them seemed to still. Her nipples tightened. An unwanted stirring started low in his groin.

"Bastard!" she hissed.

He moved his hand away. "Sorry."

"Pervert. I am not going to have sex with you!"

"Certainly not at the moment," he agreed, wishing he felt as complacent as he sounded.

Melanie resumed her struggles and it was all Roderick could do to hold her without hurting her. He patted her down, trying to be detached as he circled the waistband of her slacks and followed the path down her hips and thighs, dodging more kicks in the process.

"This would go a lot easier if you'd hold still."

He blocked the knee she aimed at his groin just in time.

"Have it your way." He turned her away from him. "Bend over the desk."

"I'll kill you!"

"That's exactly what I'm trying to prevent," he told her, dragging her hands behind her back and forcing her down over the desk. It was hard to stay objective and impersonal while running his hand over every inch of her body. It was even harder to keep from hurting her despite his advantage of height and strength. She had no compunction about trying to hurt him. His shins and toes took a beating as she fought him every inch of the way. Still, he made certain there was no gun or other weapon strapped to her legs, chest or waist. As angry as she was, she'd use one on him if she could.

The pocket of her pants yielded her cell phone, some small tools and a key ring with several keys. She nearly pulled free when he removed them and tossed them onto the desk.

In her coat pocket he found the key she had taken from the envelope in Carl's office. There was also a man's handkerchief and a comb she had appropriated from the guest room of his town house.

Abruptly, Melanie stopped struggling. Her eyes burned with fury as the other coat pocket yielded a pocketknife, her gloves, and what he assumed were Carl's keys and his security card.

Releasing her, Roderick stepped back quickly, shoving the keys and security card into his own pocket. She straightened immediately, breathing hard. Her face was flushed more from anger than exertion. He lifted the tool kit and scowled as he realized what it contained. "Lock picks?"

Arms crossed, she glared her defiance.

"So you lied. You really are a professional thief."

She remained mute and still. Quiet rage built inside him. He realized on some level he'd been hoping she would turn out to be a cook, not a thief.

"Who are you working for? I want the name, Melanie."

She said nothing. He ran through a mental list of competitors, trying to decide which one would be brazen enough—and desperate enough—to send in a thief to raid his R & D offices. What had someone wanted badly enough to risk this sort of trouble?

"It's over, Melanie," he said gruffly. "You're going to jail, you know that." The words left a bad taste in his mouth. "You may as well tell me who employed you."

He'd expected the flash of fear he saw, but not the surge of anger that followed.

"You have a nerve calling me a thief when you built your entire company on the work you steal from others."

Cold chilled his gut. "What are you talking about?"

"As if you didn't know. You and Carl Boswell—"

She trembled visibly with emotion. For a second he thought she was going to launch herself at him physically.

"—you're nothing but a clutch of thieves. At least I'm an honest thief. I only take back what belongs to me and mine."

"Explain," he demanded harshly.

"You know exactly what I'm talking about."

"No. I don't."

She reached behind her and snatched up the manila envelope. She waved it in his face.

"I suppose you know nothing about this."

"I'd have to see the contents first," he said calmly. But Melanie wasn't listening. Words tumbled past her lips with a life of their own as she pushed out her rage and frustration.

"My brother spent months developing this program! He could have taken it anywhere, but he came to RAL because of the company's reputation."

There were tears in her eyes. She was quaking with emotion.

"What a joke. I don't know what you did to him, but I know you sent Boswell to steal his program. And you aren't going to get away with it, do you hear me? I won't let you! You can have me arrested, but I'll go to the press until someone listens to me!"

Roderick forced his tone to remain calm and controlled, but inwardly, the ice spread until he felt colder than the temperature outside.

"First a sister, now a brother?"

"You bastard!"

He saw the charge coming before she leaped at him. Twisting to one side, he grabbed her around the waist and spun her harmlessly, yanking the envelope from her upraised fist. He stepped out of range before she could turn on him again.

"I have no idea what you're talking about, but RAL has never stolen from anyone. Let's see what this is all about."

Two DVDs slid from the packet into his hands. He ignored them to skim the papers. His sick feeling intensified as he scanned the cover letter, and he jumped to the signature line. Gary Andrews.

The telephone in the outer office began to ring. "Wait here," he ordered. Pete was the only one who knew Roderick was here.

Replacing the DVDs and the papers, he strode to the outer office and answered the line on his secretary's desk. "Laughlin."

"Sir, it's Pete. The police are here. The home office decided to report my call. The officers want to have a quick look around. I thought you should know."

"Thanks, Pete. I'm packing to leave right now. Will they want to talk to me?"

"I don't think so, sir. Just a minute." There was a muffled pause as he spoke with someone else. "Sir, the officer said he doesn't need to talk to you, but I'm to wait here for you to come down in the elevator."

"All right, Pete. I'll be right there." He replaced the receiver, unsurprised to find Melanie standing in the doorway. "The police are here."

"And you didn't tell them to come and arrest me?"

"Don't make me regret that decision."

She stepped aside as he reentered his office. The items he had taken from her pockets had disappeared from his desk, including the lock pick set. He made no comment, knowing she'd go wherever the manila envelope went since it appeared to be what she'd come here to get.

"We're going to finish our talk where we won't be interrupted," he told her.

"Why?"

"Looking a gift horse in the mouth?"

"When it comes with strings," she replied.

Roderick didn't respond. She watched him tidy the office and pull a large file folder from the cherry cabinet across the room. She tensed, but remained mute as he set the manila envelope underneath.

"Get your boots. And be sure to wipe the sink dry."

For a minute he thought she'd ignore the command, but she disappeared into the bathroom while he made sure he hadn't overlooked anything besides the mashed sandwich lying under his desk, where it had been kicked during their scuffle.

"Let's go," he told her when she reappeared.

"Go where?"

"We'll take the elevator."

"What happens when we reach the lobby?"

"I haven't gotten that far yet."

"Comforting," she assured him.

He locked the outer office and summoned the elevator. While they waited, he decided on a simple plan. Melanie listened, donning her hat and wrapping the scarf around her face.

"I hope that lawyer of yours is as good as you think," she muttered. "Because this is never going to work."

"You have a better idea?"

"Nope."

"Okay then. Stay directly behind the panel out of sight when the doors open. I'll block Pete's view with my body. The minute I drop the papers, go around the corner and use the side exit. You don't need the key card to get out, but you will have to go around the building. The Mercedes is in the parking lot out back."

"I don't suppose you'd give me the car keys."

"I don't suppose I would."

"Didn't think so."

Everything went as planned when the doors opened except that Pete wasn't there to appreciate the choreography.

Melanie sprinted for the corner as Roderick bent to retrieve the papers he had scattered over the marble floor as a distraction. Seconds later Pete hurried forward from the opposite corridor.

"Here, Mr. Laughlin, let me give you a hand."

"That's all right, I've got them, Pete."

"Sorry, but I heard something down that hallway," Pete said, indicating the direction from which he had come. "A broom fell over in the janitor's closet."

Roderick stilled. "A broom?"

"Yes, sir. It made quite a clatter. I know what you're thinking. I thought the same thing, but there was no sign anyone helped it fall. Still, I'm glad those two officers showed up."

"Maybe I should hang around," Roderick suggested.

"No, sir, I think it's better that you leave. If someone is in here that shouldn't be, I'd just as soon not have a civilian in the line of fire."

Roderick thought about reminding the other man that Pete was no longer wearing a police uniform, but settled for buttoning his coat instead.

"Try not to shoot holes in the marble, Pete."

"No, sir," he replied with a grin.

"Do me a favor and leave a message on my answering machine with the results of your search."

"I'll be happy to do that, sir." Pete walked him to the door, holding it open while adding a warning for Roderick to be careful driving. The reason was obvious. The winter storm was back to full force once more. Wind howled between the buildings, whipping the snow before it. Snow and frigid air pelted him.

Roderick forged toward the parking lot with his head down. At least he didn't need to worry that Melanie would leave a path to the car—assuming she actually headed for the parking lot and didn't decide to take off.

That worry was put to rest the minute he saw the car. She was there all right. So was a white van used by the security company. More reinforcements had arrived.

Chapter Seven

Two burly guards were questioning Melanie. Thanks to the swirling snow they didn't notice Roderick until he was practically right beside them.

"What seems to be the problem here?" he demanded authoritatively. Both men spun in surprise. He didn't recognize either one, but their thick winter jackets bore the familiar uniform patch.

"Who are you?" The younger of the two demanded. At the same time, the older guard ordered Roderick to stay where he was.

"Roderick Laughlin," he told them in a tone more icy than the storm. "CEO and president of RAL. This young lady is a friend of mine."

He flicked snow from his lashes as he held their gazes. The younger man holding Melanie released her as though burned. His partner wasn't as easily intimidated.

"Huh. Let's see some identification," he demanded. "Your friend claims she doesn't have any with her."

Roderick didn't spare her a glance. "I'm sure she doesn't. We left in such a hurry she forgot to bring her purse."

Roderick fished his keys from his coat pocket and pressed the button to unlock the car doors.

"Get in before you freeze to death," he told Melanie.

The young man started to protest, but stopped as Roderick leveled him with a look.

"It's too cold to be standing around out here," Roderick said.

Melanie moved closer to the car door. The younger guard let his hand drop to the club at his side.

"Fortunately, I never go anywhere without my wallet," Roderick told them.

With slow deliberation, Roderick reached under his coat for his pants pocket. His fingers closed over empty air.

"No wallet?" the guard asked in a neutral tone that grated on Roderick's stretched nerves. And in that second, he knew exactly where his wallet was.

He'd gone past the urge to shake her. He'd beat her, he decided. Hoping his smile didn't look as feral as it felt, he looked at Melanie. The only features showing between the hat and scarf were her eyes. Both held a puckish expression.

"You wouldn't happen to have my wallet, would you...darling?"

Pure mischief sparked in those china-blue eyes. "Why, yes, sweetheart," she cooed. "I picked it up in the elevator."

With effort, he suppressed the growl that rumbled low in his chest as she extended his wallet in one gloved hand. Giving her a look that promised retaliation, he wondered why no one had beaten her as a child.

Fishing out his driver's license, he handed it to the older man who examined it closely before handing it back.

"Sorry, Mr. Laughlin, but we spotted this lady here skulking around the car and we had to check it out."

"I was trying to explain to them that I locked myself out," Melanie said quickly, "but they didn't want to listen."

Roderick waved aside the apology. "I understand completely and I laud your dedication to duty. However, you should know that two police officers are inside the building with Pete Hubbard who is alone on the lower level. Only moments ago, a broom mysteriously fell over in the janitor's closet."

The younger man nodded. "We heard him call it in."

The older, more experienced guard gave his partner a look that made him blush.

"Then you'll understand why I am concerned that there may actually be an intruder inside. I'd like both of your names, please."

The men stiffened defensively, but the older man offered their names in a flat tone.

"Thank you. I want to let your boss know how pleased I am with the job you are doing. Now, let's all get where we need to go before we freeze to death."

The men relaxed. "Thank you, sir. Let us get the chain for you."

Roderick inclined his head and slid into the car. Mel followed his lead. She grinned beneath her scarf as she drew her seat belt across her chest.

"Told you few people could stand up to your brand of intimidation. It was nice of you to add that last bit. They don't deserve a reprimand for doing their job."

"No," he said in obvious warning. "*They* don't."

Uh-oh. There was no doubt about who he thought needed the reprimand. Sadly, he was right. Taking his wallet again had been an impulsive act of retaliation that had been petty and childish. She shouldn't have done it, but he was so stuffy—so certain of himself and the respect he considered his due. Mel watched covertly as he put the car in gear.

"You do realize when they check the security tapes they are going to know you were inside the building with me," he said.

His casual tone didn't fool her. He was angry and with good reason.

"I'm sorry. They're going to ask questions."

"I can handle the questions, Melanie. It's my building and my offices you burgled. However, I'd like to know why. I've earned that right, don't you think?"

As they pulled onto the street, the car immediately slid on a patch of ice and all conversation came to a halt. Roderick steered calmly into the skid until he regained control. Mel sat up straighter, afraid to breathe as wind and snow buffeted the vehicle. Visibility was nonexistent. She had known the weather conditions were horrible, but she hadn't considered how dangerous it would be to drive on barely plowed roads.

Roderick interrupted the well of silence. "We aren't going to make it back to my place." His gloved hands gripped the steering wheel, the only outward indication of his tension.

Mel leaned forward and strained to read the street signs. "Turn right at the next light," she said.

Roderick didn't take his eyes from the road. "Why?"

"My apartment is closer," she told him reluctantly.

Without a word, he turned at the intersection. The side street proved even worse. There wasn't another moving vehicle in sight. Cars were parked or simply abandoned, making navigation that much worse.

"Be careful!" she cried as the car started to slide.

Roderick swore as they nearly sideswiped an almost invisible parked car that protruded into their lane.

"How much farther?" he demanded.

"There's a parking garage the next street over. We can leave the car there and walk the rest of the way."

She held her breath as he tried to make the turn. Traction gave up the ghost and the Mercedes fishtailed. Roderick fought for control. He was winning when another patch of ice spun the heavy car in a complete circle across the road. The front fender located a utility pole with a crunch that tripped the car's air bag system, throwing them forward against the seat belts.

"Melanie! Are you all right?"

"If I don't suffocate. What's all this white powder?"

"Part of the bag's deployment system," he told her. "Are *you* all right?"

"Yes," he said tersely.

Mel tussled with the seat belt release until it clicked free. Roderick turned off the engine. Wind wrenched the door from her hand, sucking the air from her lungs as she stepped from the car. Rocky from the accident, she clung to the door with both hands and watched Roderick struggle to open his crumpled door. Finally, he gave up and climbed across the seat to join her. Standing, he braced both hands against the car roof. Their gazes locked. She would swear he looked embarrassed.

"It wasn't your fault."

"I'm well aware of that."

"Hey, it wasn't my fault, either. I tried to get you to go home, remember?"

He shut his eyes and didn't respond.

"Are you sure you're okay?" she asked nervously.

"Yes."

He opened his eyes slowly. As if he wasn't entirely steady on his feet, he moved around to the front of the car to study the bumper and the pole it had mated with. He surveyed the damage, his expression hardening. The pole swayed ominously.

"We should move. The wind could bring that down any minute."

His gaze swept the empty street. Mel shivered. The cold knifed through her coat as if she weren't wearing one. She was thankful for the scarf covering most of her face.

"How do we get to your place?"

Her hand shook as she pointed in the direction of her apartment building. Roderick opened the rear passenger door and leaned in to withdraw her duffel bag and the manila envelope from the back seat. He stuffed the envelope inside the bag before pulling up the collar of his coat around his neck.

"Lead the way."

"What about your car?"

Roderick removed his ignition key and left it under the floor mat.

"Someone will either come along to steal it or tow it." He shrugged. "Let's go."

Mel couldn't think of a response to that matter-of-fact assessment. Which was probably just as well since she soon discovered she needed every breath to plod through the drifting snow. Walking was nearly as dangerous as driving had been. If Roderick hadn't been with her, she would have taken more than one nasty spill, but his strong hand was always there to steady her.

Cutting through the parking garage gave them a respite from the snow and wind, but not the bitter cold. Roderick's face turned a ruddy deep pink and as soon as they stepped back out onto the next street over, snow once more covered his hair like a cap, turning his eyebrows white, as well. Despite her gloves and boots, Mel's fingers and toes were numb and her skin stung where it was exposed. Roderick had to be suffering far more than she was but he moved on in stoic silence.

She breathed a sigh of relief when her building finally loomed before them. If her apartment was still being watched, so be it. No one could see farther than a hand's length from their face anyhow.

Rather than hunt for her key, she pushed the button for Claire's apartment.

"Yes?" came the tinny voice.

"It's Mel."

Claire buzzed them inside.

The forced-air heat that greeted them brought their skin painfully to life. Roderick stomped snow from his boots and peered at his surroundings. Ruefully, Mel realized this was far from the sort of place he was used to visiting. The building was old and not maintained as well as it could have been, but it had heat and electricity, and at the moment, she couldn't think of anything more important.

Claire Bradshaw waited for them in the upstairs hall. Her lined features were drawn in concern that only deepened when she saw them. Her gaze immediately slid to the man behind Mel.

"Are you all right?" she asked without taking her eyes from Roderick.

Mel nodded.

"Come inside and get those wet things off right away." She ushered them into her cozy, warm apartment.

"I'm Roderick Laughlin," he told the older woman, removing his overcoat.

"Claire Bradshaw." Her white hair bobbed in satisfaction as she took his measure. "You look capable. What were you doing letting her run around out there in this weather?"

Roderick paused in the act of removing his boots. "Is there some way to control her, then?"

Claire chuckled, a hearty, infectious sound. "Not so I've noticed, now that you mention it. Here. Wrap this quilt around your legs and take off your pants."

Mel inhaled sharply. To her amazement, Roderick calmly accepted the blanket.

"Most women want a drink first."

The words were deadpan, but there was a twinkle in his dark eyes. Claire's laughter filled the apartment. She winked at Roderick while Mel gaped at the two of them.

"At my age, every minute counts and you look like a pretty prime specimen to me—much better than the wimpy types she usually has in tow."

"Is that right?"

Mel dropped her boot to the floor with a deliberate thunk. Both heads swung in her direction. She was astounded by their easy rapport.

"What are you staring at, dear?" the elderly woman asked. "Give the man a bit of privacy for heaven's sake. Go in my bedroom and finish getting undressed. I'll need to throw all your wet things in the dryer. It's unfortunate the two of you won't fit inside, as well."

Roderick smiled. It was the first time Mel had ever seen him smile and the effect was electric. It took years off his features, softening the hard lines of his face. No woman would be immune to a smile like that one.

"God knows I've been spinning in circles since I met Melanie," Roderick was saying.

"Oh, I know exactly what you mean," Claire agreed merrily.

Mel stalked to the bedroom, but not before she heard the sound of his zipper being lowered. That sound echoed in her head as she slammed the door closed behind her.

Nuts! Her mind whirled with the chaos of her thoughts. Discovering Roderick was the head of RAL had jolted her. She knew fate liked to play its little games, but of all the men in that ballroom the other night, why had it directed her to select him from the crowd? And why did he have to go and be so likable? She didn't want to like him. She couldn't afford to trust him. The man had grounds to have her arrested several times over.

But he hadn't.

She puzzled over that as she selected a heavy velour robe to put on from Claire's closet. She was so cold she wasn't sure her bones would ever feel warm again, and lethargy was stealing over her. Her thoughts were all muddled. Especially where Roderick was concerned.

He wasn't nearly as uptight as she'd believed at first. His sense of humor surprised her. But he was used to being in charge and he ran the company that had stolen from her brother. Worse, he'd called Carl Boswell his friend. What was he going to do when he found out the man was dead and she hadn't told him?

This time, her shiver wasn't entirely from the cold. Harold DiAngelis was bound to tell the police she'd been at the party. They were going to want to question her—something she had to avoid at all costs. She couldn't tell them about Gary, and how else could she explain her presence there?

Every time she thought about her brother her worry grew. What if Gary had gone to the party after all? He wasn't a violent man, but anyone could kill if the motive were strong enough.

No! Her brother had not killed Carl Boswell.

But someone had.

Roderick? Too ludicrous to consider. She'd bet anything he didn't even know the man was dead. But if Boswell hadn't tried to steal the program under orders, then what had he expected to gain? He was already a vice president, and given that pile of money in his safe, it wasn't for profit—unless that money was some of the profit.

Maybe he'd offered to sell Gary's program to one of RAL's competitors. Maybe they'd made him an offer he couldn't refuse. The thought sent her stomach plummeting.

The DVD in this envelope must be a copy. So Boswell must have turned the original over to someone at the party and was killed for his efforts. Gary was screwed.

Claire Bradshaw entered on a knock.

"Here, Mel. I slipped across the hall and brought you some clean clothing," she said. "I knew you'd be more comfortable in your own clothes and this sweatshirt looks warm."

"How'd you get into my apartment? I thought I had your spare key."

"Now dear, do you really think I only have one? Given your track record—"

"Hey, I've only lost my key a couple of times."

"And locked yourself out several other times," Claire corrected. "I'm on a first-name basis with the boy who makes the keys."

Mel stuck out her tongue and accepted the clothing. "Thanks, but you shouldn't have gone over there. What if someone is still watching the apartment?"

If her theory was correct, the watchers were connected to the killer rather than the police. They intended to silence her and her brother.

"Pshaw. No one is out there in these conditions," Claire said. "Let me have your wet things and I'll toss them in the dryer as soon as Roderick's pants are dry."

Mel forced herself to focus on her neighbor. "How am I going to repay you?"

A smile lit her lined features.

"You do that every day, darlin'. You're the daughter I never had. I'm just happy for a chance to repay you for a change. And I like your young man. This time, I think you picked a winner."

"He's not my young man," she protested instantly. "He's the one whose house I broke into last night."

"Yes, I recognized the name. I must say, your taste is definitely improving."

"Claire!"

Half an hour later, Roderick, dressed in his now-dry pants, held out a chair to seat Claire and then Mel at the small, round table in the dining area off the kitchen. The courtly gesture was so unexpected Mel hesitated. Never in living memory had a man held a chair for her and she suspected Roderick knew it. Fighting a blush, she sat down, inhaling the spicy scent of Claire's chili.

Mel would take bets that eating homemade chili in a run-down apartment building was something Roderick had never done in his life, yet he seemed perfectly at home and was not the least bit condescending.

It was Mel who felt uncomfortable. She wasn't exactly sure when she'd started thinking about how attractive Roderick was, but the unwanted awareness only made the awkward situation worse. He didn't think she was cute much less beautiful and he was right. She'd never be competition for someone like Shereen Oro. And what did it matter anyhow? Mel had a lot more important things to think about. Like why Gary wasn't answering his cell phone.

"May I ask how you two came to be together?" Claire asked as Mel forced herself to eat.

"It's a long story," Mel told her hastily. And one the crafty woman already knew.

"She picked my pocket," Roderick stated.

"She's impulsive like her mother, I'm afraid."

"Claire!"

Roderick paused, a spoon halfway to his mouth. "Her mother is a pickpocket, too?"

"Oh, she's retired now," Claire replied complacently, ignoring Mel. "However, at one time she was one of the best in the business. Married a second-story man, you know."

"No, I didn't know."

"Oh, yes. Wonderful couple."

Mel closed her eyes and prayed for a miracle. Unfortunately, it appeared she'd already used up her quota.

"Interesting career choices," Roderick said. "What about the rest of her family?"

Mel opened her eyes to glare. "Hey! I'm sitting right here, remember?"

"Yes, dear, we can see you," Claire said calmly. "Her uncle Bill—God rest his soul—was shot and killed in that bank job in Italy about seven years back, and her cousin Robby is serving five to ten in Nebraska…"

"Claire—"

"…but the rest of the family are okay. At least, I think they are. Is Margie still running that fortune-telling scam in Utah, Mel?"

Mel closed her eyes again.

"What about her brother?" Roderick inserted.

"Mel and Gary are considered the black sheep of the family, I'm afraid. Boringly normal, if you know what I mean. A shame, really. All that talent going to waste."

Mel opened her eyes once more and stared at her friend. Claire was up to something.

"What's your relationship to Melanie?" Roderick asked.

"Her mother and I grew up together. We worked the streets as a team until she met Mel's father. It was love at first sight."

Roderick didn't bat an eye at this revelation. "Do you still pick pockets for a living?"

"Oh my, no. Got caught one time with my hand in a gentleman's pocket. Turned out I'd picked the wrong mark. He'd just been laid off and was poorer than me. Married him three weeks later. We had forty-two blissful years before the cancer took him. He was a wonderful man, wasn't he, Mel? A locksmith, by trade."

Roderick sat back, looking bemused.

"More chili, dear?"

BEING WITH MELANIE was like riding a roller coaster. All twists and turns with uphill climbs that sent him plummeting to the bottom at dizzying speeds. Roderick couldn't even begin to imagine the sort of childhood she must have had, but Claire had confirmed that Melanie did indeed have a brother. Gary Andrews had submitted that query letter, so Melanie had told him the truth—or at least what she believed to be the truth. Roderick wasn't willing to grant her more than that. Carl had been his friend and a loyal employee for years. There had to be more to this.

Claire insisted the two of them move into the living room after they finished their meal. She refused his offer to help with the dishes.

"Pshaw. A couple of bowls and spoons. Besides, Mel knows I don't like anyone messing about in my kitchen. For one thing, there isn't room. For another, the two of you have some talking to do and the day isn't getting any younger. If I were you," she said turning to Melanie, "I'd trust him. He's got kind eyes."

Melanie's eyes were jewel-bright as she slumped into the overstuffed chair in the corner. Her small chin jutted forth and her body language stated plainly that she was ready for war.

"Interesting family you have," he told her mildly. "Why don't you tell me about your brother."

Her muscles relaxed slightly. She sat back and a rush of satisfaction swept over him. She was going to trust him.

"Gary's a computer technician for a small firm in Virginia. In his off-hours, he's been developing a computer program. He believes it will revolutionize the security industry."

"In what way?"

"I'm not real clear on the details," she admitted. "I'm computer-challenged so it didn't make a lot of sense to me. I just know he's been really excited about the program."

Roderick crossed to the duffel bag Claire had placed on top of a flattened plastic bag near the closet. The melting snow had left puddles. He removed the envelope Mel had taken from Carl's safe. Moving aside an onyx chessboard, he turned out the contents on the heavy wood coffee table.

His gut tightened. One of the DVDs had a label with Gary's name and phone number, further confirming her story. The other had no markings at all.

"That's the demo he sent your company," Mel said. "Carl Boswell called and expressed interest on behalf of your company. Gary was really excited. He offered to give

Boswell a full demonstration. Boswell went to Gary's apartment and told him the company was definitely interested, but Gary didn't like the offer Boswell made."

She sighed. "Look, I know he set his expectations too high. He was hoping your firm would hire him as a programmer. I told him you probably wouldn't since everyone wants college graduates these days no matter what a person can do. Still, if the money had been good enough, Gary would have sold him the program. The next thing I knew, Gary called to tell me Boswell had stolen the DVD and was planning to pass it to someone at a New Year's Eve party."

Roderick wanted to deny that allegation immediately. Only the evidence on the coffee table and the fact that she obviously believed every word kept him silent. The story wasn't a total fabrication, but it did have holes you could drive a truck through.

"If he believed that, why did your brother send you to the party? Why didn't he go himself?"

"Because your *friend* knifed him when Gary caught him in the act."

That allegation he couldn't ignore. "Impossible! I've known Carl Boswell for more than twelve years. There's no way I'm going to believe he attacked your brother."

Anger glittered in her eyes, but he didn't give her a chance to speak. "If any of this is true, why didn't your brother call the police and have Carl arrested?"

Melanie bit down on her lip and looked away. "He couldn't."

"Why not?"

"Tell him, dear," Claire said softly, coming to stand in the room.

Melanie gazed at the older woman in consternation. "I can't!"

"No, I guess you can't." Claire looked at Roderick. "But I can."

"No, Claire!"

"Her brother wasn't always a black sheep. He's wanted in California."

"Claire! Don't!"

"Roderick has to know everything if he's going to help you, Mel. You know that."

"And if he turns Gary over to the police? For God's sake, Claire, Boswell worked for him! The two of them were friends. What if Roderick is behind the theft?"

Claire tsk-tsked at her. "You don't believe that any more than I do, Mel."

Melanie lowered her gaze, confirming Claire's assertion, but it didn't make Roderick feel any better. He was hammered by conflicting emotions. Claire captured his gaze.

"Everyone makes mistakes," she said with quiet force as though reading his mind. "Even good people do dumb things. Now I'm going to the bedroom to watch a program I want to see on television while you two hash this out. I don't figure you got where you are today by making snap decisions, Roderick. And you," she said turning to Melanie, "need to remember that there are always two sides to every story."

For several minutes after Claire left the room, neither of them said anything at all. Roderick reached for the letter Gary had sent his company. "Your friend is a wise woman."

"I know."

"You're close to your brother, aren't you?"

"Aren't you close to your sister?"

"Of course." Roderick frowned thinking about his relationship with his much younger sister. "But I wouldn't lie to protect her," he said carefully, "and I certainly wouldn't send her out to do something illegal to protect my own neck."

He waited for her anger. Angry people revealed more than people in control, but once again Melanie surprised him. The anger was there all right, smoldering in the depths of her eyes, but a steely calm overlaid that anger.

"I almost feel sorry for you, *Roddy*. You keep everyone at an emotional distance, don't you? Even your poor sister, I'll bet."

Her words were close enough to the truth to bite.

"Well, my brother has always been there for me and he's never asked for anything in return until now. From your stratosphere what he asked may have seemed dangerous and illegal, but it wasn't. It isn't illegal to recover something that belongs to you and I may not be as deft as my mother, but I do know how to pick a pocket without getting caught. If your friend had had that DVD on him," she nodded to the unmarked circle, "this conversation wouldn't be taking place."

"Doesn't the fact that he didn't have it on him mean maybe your brother was wrong?"

"How can you ask that with the evidence sitting right there in front of us?"

He looked at the items on the coffee table.

"Have you got a computer?"

Chapter Eight

"No computer?" Roderick asked skeptically.

Mel shrugged. "Not one that works. Gary wanted to give me a new one after that miserable machine crashed and ate all my recipes, but I decided it wasn't worth the trouble. I have better ways to waste my time." Her eyes narrowed at his expression. "It's not funny."

"No," he agreed, all hint of amusement disappearing. "But I need a computer to read this DVD. What about Claire?"

This time it was Mel who nearly smiled. "She claims the devil created telephones, television and computers. I'll let you guess which two she has."

Roderick leaned back with a frown and pinched the bridge of his nose.

"Headache?"

"I'm fine."

She wondered if he ever willingly surrendered that iron control. It didn't seem likely. Standing, she started for the hall.

"Where are you going?" he asked.

"To get you an aspirin."

"I told you, I'm fine."

"Liar."

"What did you say?" The words seemed to drop into a sudden quiet.

"I called you a liar," she responded bravely. "Your eyes are dilated, your brow is furrowed, and you keep rubbing your temples or pinching your nose like you did last night. You have a headache."

She refused to be daunted by his dark expression. "Only a man or a fool would suffer in silence when there's no need."

To her surprise, instead of responding he reached out and plucked the white queen from the chessboard. The unexpected move focused her gaze on the ornately carved onyx piece as he twisted it between his fingers.

"This set is quite beautiful. Do you play?"

Puzzled, she nodded.

"Then you know what a powerful piece the queen is. Bold and brazen, it often comes down to her challenge at the end of a game."

His eyes lifted, nailing her feet to the floor. His thumb rubbed the polished onyx with slow, sensuous strokes.

"You've been challenging me since we met."

It was surprisingly difficult to pull her gaze from the mesmerizing movement of those long, masculine fingers.

"Now you're a king? I thought you fancied the role of a prince rescuing a damsel in distress."

His expression darkened and she suspected she'd hit a nerve. She rushed on before he could speak. "Just remember, it's your company that started playing games. Don't blame me if the pawn you tried to take out called for the queen to back him up. In case you hadn't noticed, I'm an aggressive player."

The atmosphere of the room charged with a whole new tension. His eyes held some emotion she couldn't decipher. A shiver of apprehension swept her.

"Are you aggressive in every game you play?" he asked.

The words weren't suggestive, but the tone definitely was. She lifted her chin with false bravado. Inside she quaked with strange anticipation.

"I play to win," she managed.

"So do I, Melanie."

He held her transfixed with his stare. If she gave in to the sensual pull he exerted, she would lose.

"Mel," she stated firmly.

For a minute that lasted entirely too long he stared at her without speaking. When he stood, the room shrank, isolating the two of them in a space with hardly any air at all.

Mel shook her head to break the spell. Oh, the wizard had intimidation down to an art form, all right. It took all her courage to hold her ground as he deliberately crossed the short distance that spanned them.

Roderick came to a towering stop only inches away. He extended the white queen in the palm of his hand. Automatically, her trembling fingers closed over the piece. He snared her hand, trapping it inside the incredible warmth of his palm. His grip was firm, but not hurtful. She could pull away.

Why didn't she?

His wizard's gaze held hers captive as he stroked the skin on the back of her hand lightly with his thumb—the same way he had stroked the queen only moments ago.

Mel inhaled sharply at what that intimate touch implied. The chess piece fell to the floor at their feet unnoticed.

"On second thought," he said quietly, "I will take that aspirin."

It took her brain far too long to make sense of those words. His lips curved knowingly.

"When we get this mess settled, Melanie, I think I'd very much like to see you in that green dress again."

Heat fanned the flames of her imagination. He wanted her! The knowledge was electrifying. Her body ignited while her brain went numb. Roderick was a man used to getting what he wanted—and he wanted *her.*

Mel pulled her hand free. She couldn't think of a thing to say, so she fled the room without a backward glance. If his intention had been to rattle her, he'd succeeded brilliantly.

The privacy of the bathroom offered her a chance to steady flustered nerves. Her reflection in the mirror over the sink was flushed. Wide blue eyes glittered with the images her mind was supplying.

Roderick was toying with her—amusing himself at her expense. He'd manipulated her and she'd fallen into his trap. He'd told her himself that she wasn't pretty and she wasn't cute, yet he'd sensed her attraction and used it to make her believe that he could want her.

Mel closed her eyes, surprised how that knowledge cut. She wanted him to want her. A foolish fantasy—she knew that. She wasn't vain and she had few illusions about herself, but she wasn't unattractive. In fact, when she really worked at it, the opposite was true. In her opinion, attraction was more about attitude than looks anyhow.

She gripped the basin. All right, she could turn up the charm, play the helpless Cinderella to his egotistical Prince Charming. She'd do whatever it took to enlist his help because the authorities would listen to a man like Roderick.

Of course, the plan wasn't without its risks. Trying to control a master wizard like Roderick was just asking for trouble. Still, getting her brother and herself out of this mess was all that counted.

She made a wry face at the mirror. Wizard or prince, when it came right down to it, Roderick was just a man. She knew lots of ways to handle a man. Even a powerful one like Roderick Laughlin III.

When she returned to the living room she saw that the chess piece was back on the board and Roderick was in Claire's favorite chair studying the papers he'd taken from the envelope. He was squinting, she noticed. Was that due to his headache or did he need reading glasses? Unkindly, she hoped it was the latter. There was a trace of reassurance in the idea that Roderick might have a common flaw.

He looked up, his expression pensive. All the earlier signs of seduction were gone.

"Have you talked to your brother since last night?"

Remembering her earlier attempts to reach Gary by cell phone she shook her head as she set the aspirin bottle on the table within his reach. "I'll get you some water."

"I can get it," he said peevishly.

"I'm up."

His mood change was unsettling. Was this part of his strategy to keep her off balance? She half expected him to touch her hand again when she returned with the water, but he took the glass with a simple thank-you and swallowed down two tablets he'd removed from the bottle.

"I'm surprised you didn't go to your brother if he's as badly hurt as you implied," he said.

The words stung as she suspected they were meant to. "In case you forgot, it's snowing out there."

"I meant last night," he corrected mildly. "I would have expected you to rush to check on him when he first told you he was hurt."

Darn the man. He was too perceptive. She turned away and crossed to the opposite chair.

"You did, didn't you?" he persisted.

There was nothing to be gained by denying it. She hadn't even told Claire that she'd gone to Gary's apartment right after he'd called.

"Gary was gone. The front door was unlocked and the apartment was a wreck. Gary's compulsively neat. Anyone could see there had been a fight. There was a bloody washcloth in the bathroom." Her stomach tightened at the memory of the dark wet blood. "I've tried to call him a number of times since then but his cell phone is turned off." She swallowed the acid taste of fear. Where was he? Why hadn't he called her yet?

"Maybe he went to the hospital."

"He wouldn't. He'd have to explain how he came to be hurt."

"And he wouldn't want to draw attention to himself," Roderick added thoughtfully. "What about friends?"

"Gary wouldn't involve an outsider in a situation like this any more than I would."

"Just his baby sister, huh?"

The gruffness in Roderick's tone made her bristle. "What makes you think I'm his *baby* sister?"

"You told me as much earlier."

She'd forgotten. Angry, but not sure exactly why, she stood and began to pace.

"What aren't you telling me, Melanie?"

She tried to cover her guilty start with a glare. "What do you mean?"

"Don't ever play poker. What else did you find at your brother's place?"

She was so relieved at the direction of the question that she shook her head. "Nothing."

He waited expectantly.

"I didn't have much time to look around. Two men broke in while I was there."

The oath he uttered was soft, but fervent.

"It's okay, they didn't see me. I hid in the bathtub behind the shower curtain." She shoved at her hair nervously. "The key to hiding in a bathtub successfully is to leave the shower curtain pulled back part way. If it's closed all the way, people tend to look behind it."

His dark expression would have been much worse if he'd known that one of the men had entered the bathroom and lifted the washrag. She'd seen his hand clearly. If the mirror had been positioned differently, or if he had taken the time to peer around the edge of the shower curtain…but it wasn't and he hadn't. He didn't see her and she didn't see him. She had stood there on legs of jelly, quaking until she heard the front door shut. Even then, it had taken all her courage to leave the apartment.

"Who were they?" Roderick demanded.

"They weren't in the mood to announce their names to the empty apartment," she said acerbically to cover the remembered fear. No doubt they were the same men who had chased her through the ballroom—the same men who had arrived at her apartment last night. Until now, she hadn't thought about where they fit into things.

"Rivals of yours, maybe?" she suggested.

As she considered the possibility she decided it made sense.

Roderick rubbed his chin thoughtfully. "Who did your brother query besides RAL?"

"I don't know. He only talked about sending the demo to your firm."

Roderick considered that. "So who were you running from at the party?"

The uncanny leap made her squirm. "I thought they were hotel security," she told him honestly. "But now I wonder if they were the men who broke into my brother's place. That would explain how they got here so fast afterward. They went through Gary's papers. They could have found my name and address there."

"They came here?"

"Why do you think I went to your place to hide? They staked out my apartment."

"They must think you have the DVD." Roderick rose to his feet and strode to the window overlooking the street.

"Don't worry," she said as he pulled back the heavy velvet drape. "No one was out there when we arrived. Besides, my apartment is across the hall. They'll be watching for lights or movement in there, not in here."

Roderick frowned. "Claire went over there earlier to get your clothes."

"She knows how to be careful."

Roderick dropped the drape and regarded her with his darkest look to date.

"Too bad you don't share that trait."

Mel bristled. "What's that supposed to mean?"

Instead of replying, he strode to the kitchen.

"What are you doing?" she called.

"What I should have done a long time ago. I'm going to call Carl."

Panic sent her dashing after him. "You can't!"

He lifted the receiver from the wall-mounted telephone. "Why not?"

Because he'd learn that Carl had been murdered. He'd conclude that she or her brother had killed him. And Mel couldn't shake the horribly persistent thought that maybe Gary *had* killed Boswell. But then he would have had to go to the party and he wouldn't have sent her. She didn't believe it. Still, the slim possibility did exist no matter how much she wanted to deny it.

Pushing those thoughts aside between one blink and another, she addressed Roderick. "Boswell won't tell you the truth," she said desperately. "If you tip him off, he's going to lie and cover up evidence."

"*We* have the evidence," Roderick reminded her.

"Wouldn't it be better to talk to him face-to-face?"

"What are you afraid of, Melanie?"

She broke eye contact and took a steadying breath. The temptation to tell him everything practically choked her. Only loyalty to her brother kept her silent.

"I won't let you send my brother to prison! He made a mistake years ago when he was young and stupid. He got caught before they stole anything, no one got hurt, and he learned from his mistake. He never did anything illegal again. He doesn't deserve to go to jail because of a stupid dare!"

Roderick put down the receiver. "He tried to rob someone on a dare?"

Mel bit her lip, wishing she could call the words back. Miserably, she nodded. "My cousin dared him into going along when he broke into a rich classmate's home. The family was supposed to be away for the weekend. They weren't."

"Would this be the same cousin who's serving time in Nebraska?"

"His brother," she admitted.

Roderick rubbed his jaw.

"You've got as big a stake in our current situation as I have," she said desperately. "Gary's a good man. His reputation means every bit as much to me as your company's reputation does to you. You already trust Boswell. Wouldn't you like to hear Gary's side from his own lips?"

Roderick's eyes narrowed as he considered that. Sensing victory, Mel pressed home her point. "Sooner or later, Gary will call to see if I succeeded." She would not consider that he might be unable. "I'll arrange for you two to meet. Just hear him out first, that's all I'm asking."

"And what if I don't like what I hear, Melanie? What if the situation isn't what you believe?"

"That envelope is proof enough for me. You've read his letter."

Roderick pinched the bridge of his nose. He seemed to realize what he was doing and dropped his hand to his side.

"There are other explanations, you know. If your brother's program can deliver what he claims—"

"You were impressed!" she exclaimed.

"That remains to be seen."

"Gary's brilliant. You'll see. Who knows more about getting around a security system than someone who grew up surrounded by professional thieves? Please, you have to talk to Gary first."

Amusement vied with vexation as he regarded her. "What if he doesn't call?"

"He'll call." He had to call.

"And what do you propose we do to fill in the time while we wait?"

There went her imagination again, off on one of its totally irrational tangents.

"Chess?"

FROM HIS PERCH ON THE EDGE of the couch, Roderick frowned at the chessboard. "That's a totally illogical move."

"Uh-huh. Mate in three."

He stared at her animated features and wondered how he could have ever considered her plain. "Impossible."

"Actually," Claire offered, knitting needles clicking, "I believe you'll have him in two, Mel."

"You're right," she said gleefully. "My queen can take his castle."

Roderick rubbed his temple, accepting defeat. "Who taught you how to play?"

"Gary. Want to play again?"

"No thanks, I know when I'm overmatched."

"You almost won the first game," she said.

"Not really." He rolled his shoulders and his fingers went to his temples.

"Do you have a headache, Roderick?" Claire asked setting her knitting to one side. "I have aspirin."

"I already took some, thank you. It's getting late." He looked pointedly at Melanie.

She stopped resetting the pieces on the board. "He'll call."

Obviously, she was worried, as well.

"When he does, you can let me know."

Panic flared in her eyes. "Where are you going?"

"It's stopped snowing. I'm going home. It's late and I need some sleep."

"They haven't plowed the roads yet," Claire protested.

"Besides, you wrecked your car," Melanie rushed to add. "Remember?"

Roderick squeezed the bridge of his nose. He couldn't believe he'd forgotten that. The knot on the side of his head and the constant headache should have been enough to remind him.

"I could make up the couch," Claire offered with a worried expression.

Roderick considered laying his six-foot frame on the narrow, worn couch and shook his head.

"Or you could use Mel's bed," Claire continued.

Chess pieces scattered.

"No he can't!"

"Well he can hardly sleep on the floor, dear," Claire pointed out. "And my bed only sleeps two." She added a mischievous wink in Roderick's direction. "While I admit it's tempting, I doubt our guest would feel comfortable sharing the bed with me."

Roderick winked back and stepped around the table to carry his coffee cup out to the kitchen. He wasn't surprised when Mel raced after him.

"My apartment isn't safe," she protested.

Spotting the aspirin bottle now sitting on the counter, he tapped out two more tablets, filled his cup with water and swallowed them down. Melanie watched anxiously, her expression a mix of fear and something else.

He already knew she wasn't telling him everything and for the thousandth time he wondered if he'd made a mistake not calling Carl. While he trusted his friend, Carl hadn't mentioned Gary's proposal at last week's meeting—and he should have. Then there was that troubling wad of cash sitting in his safe. Roderick wanted to believe Carl had a reasonable explanation, but when added to his wife's suspicions of a lover and Roderick's own disquiet over Carl's recent actions, he'd allowed himself to be persuaded to hear her brother first.

"Why don't you take Claire's bed? She can take the couch and I'll sleep on the floor," Melanie was saying.

"Claire is not going to spend an uncomfortable night on the couch while I use her bed." Roderick punctuated his words by setting down the cup with an aggressive clunk.

"Okay, fine. You sleep on the couch."

"I won't fit."

"Then you can sleep on the floor."

"There is no reason for any of us to sleep on the floor when we have a perfectly good bed available." He raised his hand to stave off her immediate protest. "I'll keep the lights off. No one will even know I'm there. As you pointed out, it's unlikely anyone is watching the apartment tonight."

"But—"

"I'm just going to use the bed, Melanie. I'm too tired to probe your privacy."

"That isn't the point!"

"What is the point?" As she struggled for an explanation, he gave in to the temptation to bait her a little. "We could always share your bed, and give Claire back her privacy," he offered.

A choked sound came from the living room. Pink swarmed up Melanie's cheeks. For an instant he would have sworn he saw a spark of answering excitement in her eyes.

"That isn't funny. Will you be reasonable?" she pleaded.

"I believe I am. I'm going to sleep in your bed tonight with you or without you. It's only fair since you slept in mine last night."

Her eyes flashed, as he'd known they would.

"I slept in your guest room!"

He lifted her chin and felt a quiver run through her at the contact.

"What are you afraid of, Melanie?"

"Not you," she declared stoutly.

"No?"

She was so fierce. And so incredibly soft. He rubbed his thumb along the edge of her jaw.

"Stop that."

Her breathing quickened, but she didn't pull away.

"My apartment's a mess," she said breathlessly.

Roderick let her see his amusement. "I'm not the house inspector."

"You'll need clean sheets. I haven't done the laundry this week. And I don't have satin, you know. You'll get percale at my place," she added frantically.

He smiled, dropping his hand reluctantly. She reminded him of a kitten with its fur all ruffled.

"Satin sheets are highly overrated. They tend to be slippery."

Her eyes widened. He'd bet she'd never slept on satin sheets in her life.

"Not at all warm on a winter's night," he added suggestively. "Why don't you tell me what's really bothering you?"

Melanie inhaled, making him uncomfortably aware of the rise and fall of her breasts beneath the dark sweatshirt.

"For one thing, I told you, I prefer to be called Mel." Her eyes glittered defiantly.

"Too masculine. It doesn't suit you at all."

Even though he hadn't planned to touch her again, Roderick felt compelled to brush back a wispy tendril of hair that had drifted over her forehead. He shouldn't have been surprised to find her hair was as soft as her skin. Her hair invited a man's fingers to tangle in the bewitching mass. He liked that she wasn't the type to coat it with stiff hairspray.

"What are you doing?" she whispered.

An excellent question. He dropped his hand to his side.

"You're good at conversational misdirection, aren't you, Melanie?"

"Me? I'm not the one who was…" She broke off, the pink in her cheeks turning a becoming dusky rose.

The sound of Claire's needles clicking together helped Roderick throttle back the predatory urge to push the limits and watch her response. He stepped back and forced an easy smile instead. "Will it help if I promise not to pry? I'm only going to use your bed."

"I don't like it."

"We've established that."

"What if something happens?"

"Like what?" he asked, truly curious.

"What if my brother calls?"

He relaxed. "You can come and get me."

"Those men could come back."

Her persistence amused him while making him increasingly curious.

"Do you think they have a key?"

"Not everyone needs a key," she reminded him with a haughty toss of her head that drew his attention once more to her hair. Wild and unpredictable—just like her.

"Not everyone knows how to pick a lock, either," he pointed out. "You know, sooner or later you're going to run out of excuses."

Her shoulders slumped.

"You'll need a flashlight."

"In the left-hand drawer," Claire called from the living room.

Melanie sent a scowl in her direction.

"Walk over and show me where things are," he invited.

"What things?"

"Towels, soap—a razor would be nice."

"You're going to shave? Now?"

"No, not now, in the morning. I shower and shave every morning."

"Bloody heck."

He suppressed a chuckle. She was so appealing on so many levels. He couldn't resist teasing her a little more.

"It's not usually, you know."

Claire laughed out loud. Melanie grimaced.

"Fine. Sleep in my bed. What do I care?"

"That's what I've been trying to figure out."

Having accepted defeat, Melanie stalked into the living room. Claire smiled up at them.

"I'll be right back," Melanie told her grumpily.

"Take your time, dear. Sleep well, Roderick."

"Thank you. And thank you for dinner and the refuge."

"Oh, believe me, it's been my pleasure. I haven't enjoyed an evening like this in a long time. I'll see you in the morning, dear. Just come over whenever you're ready."

"I'll do that. Good night."

Melanie waited impatiently. She wouldn't meet his eyes as she quickly crossed to her own door when he followed her out of the apartment.

Anticipation tingled down his spine as she inserted her key and the dead bolt turned free.

Chapter Nine

"Take my hand," Mel ordered nervously.

Roderick slid his much larger hand into hers. "Why?"

"I don't want to chance the flashlight until we're in the back of the apartment in case someone is still watching."

His cupped his palm around her much smaller hand. Instantly, Mel realized touching him had been a mistake. The dry warmth of his skin was a sensual distraction she could have done without. Roderick exuded enough raw sexuality to make her heart thuddingly aware of him without the physical connection. And taking his hand turned out to be completely unnecessary.

Mel had forgotten how much light would be reflected off the snow outside. Her living room was tossed with plenty of illumination from the window overlooking the main street, yet he made no effort to release her hand and she was reluctant to pull away.

"My apartment's a mirror image of Claire's," she said quietly. "The bedroom's back this way."

She was pretty sure she'd left clothing strewn about in her rush to dress for the New Year's party. If only she'd taken the time to make her bed. Mel flinched from the thought while telling herself his opinion didn't matter.

This was her place. She didn't have the luxury of a maid or someone to pick up after her every day.

But that wasn't the reason she slowed her pace as she reached the short hall. The apartment had a distinctly chilled, empty feeling. It may have been due to the friendly warmth that had filled Claire's unit, but Mel felt a prickle of unease as she approached the bedroom door.

She released Roderick's hand.

"Wait," she whispered.

Roderick tensed. Mel slipped inside the familiar room, hugging the shadows while her gaze roved the space and her ears strained to hear the slightest sound.

There was nothing, yet she felt certain that someone had been in here. A shiver went straight down her spine. She turned to find Roderick filling the open doorway, a perfect silhouette.

"Fool! If someone had been in here you would have made an easy target."

"And what the devil were you planning to do, yell boo?"

"Don't be ridiculous." But she could feel a blush spreading up her neck. "You can't stay here."

"Why not?"

"Because someone was in here."

He closed the space between them, one large hand gripping her upper arm. She should have been annoyed instead of reassured by that contact.

"How do you know?"

"I just know."

She thought he'd argue. He didn't.

"Claire came over to get your clothes."

"Not Claire, someone else." She shook her head, unable to explain her unease.

"Maybe we should go to my place."

She was relieved that he took her seriously, but he obviously wasn't thinking. "How would we get there? Your car's on the side of the road, remember?"

"Don't you have a car?"

"Not one that starts in cold weather." She offered him a weak shrug. "It's not all that fond of warm weather, either. The transmission is going. It's old and crotchety."

A slow smile warmed his lips. It was amazing what a difference a smile made in those chiseled features. Even in the semi-dark she could see the way the corners of his eyes crinkled.

"Of course it is," he agreed.

He brushed back the irritating strand of hair that kept slipping down to tickle her forehead. Mel shivered at that light contact.

"Are you cold?"

"No."

On the contrary, she was heating up all too nicely. He was so close—close enough to speed the rhythm of her blood. This was bad. She needed to step away and she needed to do it now. Unfortunately, her feet weren't accepting the message.

His smile altered, taking on a sensual almost predatory appearance. His fingers lightly traced the side of her face, coming to rest at her chin, millimeters from her bottom lip. She felt it quiver as she sensed the desire growing in him.

She couldn't think.

"You are the most unusual woman."

The husky sound of his voice rippled over her. Before she could wonder at the words, his fingers lifted her chin. With tantalizing slowness, he lowered his head.

He was going to kiss her!

Her lungs forgot how to breathe.

She was going to let him!

The tension that pooled in her lower body exploded as his mouth covered hers. Hunger, shocking in its intensity, sent her arms sliding around his neck. Her lips parted to invite more intimate contact even as a tiny moan slipped from her throat.

He met her insistent demand with an answering fierceness, drawing her more tightly against the hard wall of his chest. Startled, she felt the stirring press of his erection.

His fingers glided along the skin of her abdomen beneath her blouse.

"You aren't wearing a bra," he breathed.

Mel would have told him that Claire hadn't thought to bring one over with her. She would have told him she hadn't thought it necessary beneath the thick sweatshirt. But his palm rubbed across the bare flesh of one nipple and words failed her at the incredible friction.

"What are you doing?" she managed.

His smile was definitely predatory.

"Seducing you."

"You can't!"

"No? Let's find out."

"Roderick!"

"Yes. Say my name again," he commanded huskily.

And he bent his head lower to place his mouth where his palm had been.

"Roderick!"

Mel thought she would die from the fantastic rush that melted her senses and stole her ability to remember why this was all wrong. He eased her back against the wall— a good thing since her legs had gone to mush along with her brain. Not until his fingers began to tease the elastic at her waist, did her brain reconnect.

"No!"

Roderick stopped instantly.

"No?"

"We can't!"

"Are you sure? I certainly can."

Oh, God, so could she.

"I don't sleep with men I've just met."

He brushed at her hair. Amusement laced his voice.

"I wasn't planning on a whole lot of sleep. You want me, and God knows, I want you."

He wanted her. Incredible.

With the taste of him in her mouth, the feel of him on her body, the need thrumming through her veins, it was hard to remember why they couldn't do what they both wanted to do so badly. The wall clock in the living room chimed the hour.

Mel drew a shuddery breath.

"I'm not prepared," she whispered. "Are you?"

He stilled, drawing his mouth from her skin.

"There are other ways," he said softly after a moment.

Her mind stumbled over those other ways, while her body sang agreement. Mel had no idea how she found the ability to speak.

"Is that what you want?"

His hands dropped away. Roderick stepped back and she felt bereft.

"No," he admitted gruffly, "that's not what I want. It's not what you want, either, is it?"

She couldn't summon an answer. Her body quaked with suppressed passion.

"Go back to Claire's," he ordered. "In the morning, we'll decide what to do."

"About sex?"

She bit her lip. How could she have said that? Roderick's expression was impossible to read.

"That, too."

"I—"

"Melanie, if you don't want to share your bed with me, you need to go. Right now."

Melanie went.

HIS HEADACHE RETURNED with a vengeance. Roderick couldn't believe he'd just done that. What had happened to his rigid control? Sex was wonderfully enjoyable, but he never got lost in the moment. And he never, ever forgot about something as vital as birth control. He couldn't afford to forget. A man in his position was a target. But if Melanie hadn't called a halt, he'd have had her on that bed in another minute and satisfied both their needs.

Maybe then he could have started thinking straight again.

Roderick shut the bathroom door and flicked on the light. Since the room was on an inside wall, no one would see the small shaft of light that escaped beneath the door. And if they did, well, he could use a little physical exercise right about now.

His hands clenched as he looked around the small space. A pair of plain white cotton bras hung suspended from the shower rod. Two sets of matching panties were draped over the hot and cold taps inside the tub. Simple and direct like the woman herself.

Shereen wouldn't be caught dead in such utilitarian garments. Neither would any of the women he knew.

He wondered what that said about him.

Melanie was not the sort to spend a fortune on bits of satin and lace that only a lover would see.

Did she even have a lover?

He knew next to nothing about her, but she had kissed him with wild abandon rather than the more sophisticated responses he'd come to expect.

He pulled his gaze to the vanity where a hairbrush, blow dryer and curlers were among the items littering the small area. Roderick was reminded of his younger sister. Pansy could make chaos out of order faster than anyone else he knew, but he had a feeling Melanie could hold her own.

There was very little in the way of makeup, he noted, foolishly pleased. The bright red bottle of nail polish and a tube of matching lipstick looked brand-new down to the price tags still attached. She'd bought them to go with the naughty green dress, he'd wager. Camouflage to get her inside the party.

The thought of her posing as a party girl set his teeth together. Didn't she realize how dangerous that had been?

A purple comb had fallen to the floor unnoticed. He bent to retrieve it, noting that the tile floor was clean despite the crumpled bath towel in one corner. Obviously, she'd been aiming for the full hamper and missed. He picked that up, as well. A faint, airy fragrance clung to the terry cloth. Melanie didn't drench herself in scents.

It disturbed him that he was coming to like a great deal about her.

He pulled his thoughts from that direction and debated taking a shower. His shoulders and back were tight from the earlier accident, but he knew from experience that his muscles would feel worse come morning. Better to wait. Besides, there were no fresh towels in here. In the morning, he could hunt for a linen closet without risking a light. The haphazardly hung pale green hand towel on the bar at his back would suffice for washing up tonight.

In the bedroom Roderick had to push aside a thick paperback novel to make room for his neatly folded clothing on the end of the dresser. Did she enjoy concerts and plays, as well? She probably hadn't had much opportunity to attend either one. The idea of opening those worlds to her held a lot of appeal and he gave in to the fantasy as he set about straightening the sheets and blankets. Melanie was a restless sleeper. It would be fun to see her reaction to satin sheets—if he could remember what he'd done with them.

He had to move several garments from the bed and picked up others from the floor, setting them all on a nearby chair. Melanie appeared to favor dark colors. He would have dressed her in bright, vibrant hues, definitely a blue to match her eyes.

He smiled wryly. Melanie would have plenty to say about that. He liked that she stood up for herself. Even more, he liked the way she stood up for her brother. Family loyalty was important. He only hoped it wasn't misplaced.

A yawn caught him and he climbed into her bed. One of his last conscious thoughts was that his sister would really like Melanie. The two of them would be seriously formidable if they ever got together. Pansy would take savage delight in the way Melanie pushed him through hoops. His sister was always telling him that he needed to lighten up and stop dating plastic Barbie dolls. There was certainly nothing plastic about Melanie.

RODERICK DIDN'T KNOW what woke him, but he came out of a deep sleep, instantly aware that something was wrong. The atmosphere of the small apartment had changed. He sensed that he was no longer alone.

His eyes flicked to the illuminated dial of the bedside clock. Five twenty-seven. He lay perfectly still, listening hard over the pounding of his heart.

A whisper of sound came from beyond the bedroom door.

Not Melanie. He knew it in his gut.

Quietly, he shoved aside the covers. The bed creaked betrayingly as he swung his feet to the floor. The doorway filled with a dark, solid presence.

Roderick came all the way off the bed in a silent rush. A fleeting thought reminded him that if the intruder was armed, Roderick would never get the chance to take Melanie to bed or anywhere else. Then he collided with the sinister shape.

The intruder fell back with a grunt of surprise. Roderick's fist collided with his face. As they grappled, it quickly became apparent that Roderick was operating at a serious disadvantage. He was nude while his opponent was fully dressed down to a heavy parka, boots and a ski mask.

It was the ski mask that bothered him the most. His opponent didn't intend to be recognized.

The man landed a blow that sent the air rushing from Roderick's lungs. He slumped back against the wall. Instead of seizing the advantage, the intruder whirled and sprinted for the living room. Unable to move for a minute, Roderick heard the main door open and close. He was alone in the apartment once more.

Using the wall for support, he made his way down the hall. He took a small measure of satisfaction in knowing that the first blow he'd landed would leave a mark, but he wished he could have done more.

Roderick opened the door cautiously. As expected, the hallway was empty. Melting snow had created a path that led straight to Melanie's door. The bastard had known exactly where he was going, but at least Melanie was safe. He hadn't gone near Claire's unit.

Roderick rubbed the back of his neck, trying to ease bunched muscles. He decided against letting the women know what had just happened. There was nothing they could do and there was no point waking them just to upset them.

He cursed under his breath, closed the door and relocked it. Feeling only slightly ridiculous, he hauled an overstuffed armchair over to prop against the door. It wouldn't stop anyone from entering, but it would slow them down and he'd hear the intruder before the bastard got as far as the bedroom.

Knowing the adrenaline rush would keep him from sleeping any further, Roderick headed for the bathroom. In the light over the mirror he saw that his knuckles were bruised. The skin had split in two places. He rinsed the cuts thoroughly. His stomach was tender where the punch had connected, but given that he'd been at a serious disadvantage, he figured he'd gotten off lightly. The guy could have pulverized him.

Of course, the intruder probably hadn't expected any resistance at all. Instead of a man his size, the bastard had been expecting to deal with one small, helpless woman.

Helpless?

Melanie?

Roderick made a wry face at himself in the mirror. The intruder should be grateful. Melanie probably knew karate. No doubt she would have taken the jerk down and tied him up with his own belt.

Roderick regarded his features in disgust. He should have been able to give a better accounting of himself. Being a hero was a lot harder than it looked in the movies.

He rubbed his temples. He was going to have quite a few words to say to Gary Andrews when they met. The man deserved to be beaten for putting his sister in this sort of danger.

Roderick went in search of a linen closet. In addition to towels and a package of neon-pink razors, he found half a can of unscented shaving cream and a surprisingly heavy flashlight. He weighed it with his hand. Feeling only slightly foolish, he carried it into the bathroom with him.

The shower helped work some of the stiffness out of his muscles and he discovered the blade on the razor was surprisingly sharp. He wondered if the shaving cream belonged to Melanie or was left over from someone who had stayed with her.

A sound from the living room scattered his thoughts. He turned off the water. Someone was pushing the chair from in front of the door. Grabbing the flashlight he started for the living room.

"I knew I shouldn't have let him come over here. I knew it!"

Roderick stopped as Melanie squeaked past the chair. She came to a startled halt. He realized he'd raised the hand clenching the flashlight, prepared to strike at the intruder.

He lowered the flashlight. Then he remembered he was nude.

"Sorry. I wasn't expecting you this early."

He turned around. Her shock gave way to a muffled giggle.

"Thanks," he grumbled without stopping. "That's just what a man wants to hear after he's bared his all to a woman."

"I'm sorry," she gasped around giggles. "It's just that

you're always so perfectly groomed. I never expected…
and that flashlight…talk about a fashion accessory."

Setting the flashlight down he wiped the remaining
veins of shaving cream from his face and quickly wrapped
the damp bath towel around his waist.

"You weren't who I was expecting, either."

"What do you mean? Who were you expecting?"
Melanie demanded as she appeared in the bathroom
doorway.

"Do you mind if I get dressed before we have this conversation?"

She stepped back to let him pass into the bedroom. Her
gaze went to the tidy stack of clothing on the end of her
dresser and she blushed nicely as he reached for his briefs.

"Oh."

She pivoted in embarrassment and he stepped into his
briefs, then reached for his pants.

"What did you mean about expecting someone?" she
asked again.

"You had a visitor this morning."

"What?"

She whirled around as he finished zipping his pants.

"Who?"

Her gaze went to his hands and her blush deepened. He
fastened the clip at the waistband.

"You're hurt!"

Roderick realized she was staring at his scraped knuckles.

"Your visitor wasn't expecting me."

"Ohmygod. Did he get the DVD?"

Melanie went right to the heart of the issue.

"No," he said, surprisingly annoyed. "And I wasn't seriously hurt, thank you for asking. I left your brother's pre-

cious program on Claire's coffee table last night," he reminded her.

Her color stayed high but she remained focused on his face.

"Was that what the intruder wanted?"

Roderick raised his eyebrows.

"I didn't ask, and he didn't say. We were a little busy fighting."

"You fought him? Here?"

"Right here, actually."

He reached for his shirt and winced. While the shower had felt wonderful at the time, his muscles had tightened again. This morning's altercation hadn't helped any.

"You *are* hurt!" Melanie exclaimed.

"Just stiff," he admitted. "I'm not as young as I used to be."

"Let me help you."

She reached for his shirt and brushed the firm skin of his upper arm. The contact went straight to his groin. Embarrassed by the reaction, he took a hasty step back.

She did the same, her cheeks a brilliant pink.

"I can manage," he told her, and proved it by pulling on the shirt. "Have you heard from your brother yet?"

The consternation on her face was all the answer he needed.

"He'll call! The battery on my cell phone needs charging, that's why I came over here."

And it was a measure of how badly she affected him that he hadn't even noticed the small phone clutched in her right hand.

"And also to tell you that Claire's fixing breakfast," she added quickly.

Melanie crossed to the red plastic crate that served as one of her nightstands and unplugged the charger sitting there.

"Tell Claire I'll be over as soon as I finish getting dressed."

"All right. He will call, honest."

"I'll take your word for it."

He buttoned his shirt, listening for the sound of the door. No woman had ever had such a disconcerting affect on his control before.

The minute he finished dressing he reached for his cell phone. He'd forgotten to turn it on yesterday, so it should have had plenty of charge left.

There were seven missed calls. The first was from Pansy wishing him a happy New Year. Ruefully, he realized he'd been so caught up in everything that he'd forgotten to call and check on her.

The second call was from Carl's home number. Joyce Boswell's voice filled his ear, pitched high with strain.

"Roderick! Oh, God, Roderick, where are you? He's dead. Carl's dead. The police say he was murdered! Please call me. I don't know what to do!"

Horror was a cold, gut-wrenching numbness. He'd felt like this only once before—the day they had come to tell him his family had been in an accident.

Numb, Roderick dialed the familiar number, holding his emotions under tight control. An unfamiliar male voice answered on the second ring.

"This is Roderick Laughlin. May I speak with Joyce Boswell?"

"This is Evan Quill, Mr. Laughlin," the deep voice said. "I'm Joyce's father. I know she wants to speak with you, but she finally took the sedative the doctor gave her and she's still asleep. May I give her a message?"

"I'm sorry, Mr. Quill. I wasn't thinking about the time. I just got her message. It's true then? Carl's dead?"

"I'm afraid so."

Roderick could hear the weariness in the older man's voice. Sternly, he pushed down the sea of emotions that threatened to overwhelm him.

"Can you tell me what happened?"

"Not much more than what the news has been reporting. Did you know he walked out on Joyce and the kids New Year's Eve?"

All the air left his lungs at once.

"He told her he was sorry but that he'd met someone else and he needed some time…"

The older man's voice broke before coming back more strongly.

"…time to decide what to do."

His anger was laced by bewilderment. Roderick gripped the phone more tightly.

"Joyce was devastated. She called her mother and we drove up right away. Then the police came in the middle of the night and said he'd been murdered."

Roderick felt physically ill. Guilt gnawed on his intestines. He should have done something when Joyce first came to him.

"How was he murdered?"

He sensed the other man's surprise.

"I've been out of touch since New Year's Eve," he explained raggedly. "I haven't heard any news reports."

"I see. He was shot at close range with a small-caliber gun at some private party at a hotel in D.C. New Year's Eve. A witness saw a woman in a bright green dress run from the scene. We figure it was the woman he left Joyce for. Do you have any idea who she might be?"

Melanie.

Chapter Ten

Mel paced Claire's living room restlessly. Her thoughts were so chaotic she couldn't focus on any one of them. She was worried sick about her brother. Gary should have been in touch by now.

And who had entered her apartment last night? One of the men who'd been watching the place—or could it have been Gary? What if he'd come to her for help and Roderick had chased him away? Gary would be thinking the worst. He'd think something had happened to her and someone had set a trap for him. But if it hadn't been him, then the person would be back, and this time he'd be prepared for Roderick.

Roderick.

Her mind shied from the image of him stark naked holding that ridiculous flashlight like a club. He had an incredible physique. *And she'd giggled.* How could she have giggled? It was no use telling herself that it had been a nervous reaction. She'd acted like a little girl who'd never seen a naked man before.

Mortified, she tried not to think about him. Thinking led to the memory of the way he'd kissed her and she'd spent most of the restless night reliving that moment. She was a mess and she couldn't afford to be a mess right now. She needed to concentrate. She needed a plan of action.

"You're pacing," Claire said as the front door swung open. "There's no use fretting you know. Gary's going to be just fine."

"Don't count on it," Roderick said from the open door behind her.

His countenance was so grim Mel flinched. Then she saw the cell phone in his hand. Oh, God, he knew about Boswell.

"I have to give you credit, Melanie," he said with a calm that sent splinters of fear through her stomach. "Not many people can fool me so completely."

She should have told him. But she hadn't, so she raised her chin and faced him with false calm.

"Boswell did."

For an instant, shock replaced his anger.

"I didn't kill your friend."

Claire gasped. Neither of them looked at her. Two steps brought Roderick close enough for Mel to feel the rage sheeting off him.

"You were seen, Melanie. You used *me* to escape!"

He would never forgive her for that.

"Are you going to hit me or are you going to listen?" she asked with false calm.

"To more lies?"

"Carl Boswell was dead when I found him."

For a moment she thought he was past listening, but he visibly clamped down on the rage seething in his eyes and held her gaze.

"You used me to escape," he repeated.

"Yes."

Muscles bunched in his jaw. His fingers curled, then released.

"Tell me," he commanded roughly.

Cloaking herself in false calm, Mel willed him to listen. She told him everything, because if Roderick didn't believe her now, she and her brother had no chance at all.

When she finished, the silence was so profound it beat at her ears. She held his gaze. Did he believe her? His forbidding expression gave no hint of his thoughts. The sound of a plow out front sent his glance toward the curtained windows and Mel released the breath she'd been holding.

"And you have no idea who killed him," he asked with heavy sarcasm turning back to her.

"No."

She watched him weighing her words. His hands fisted.

"Carl was a good man," he bit out. "A friend."

She hurt for his pain, but Roderick had to see beyond his friendship with the other man. He had to believe her.

"He stole Gary's program," she said forcefully. "He left my brother bleeding on the floor of his apartment."

"Tell me why I should believe a thing you've said," Roderick growled. "You've done nothing but lie to me since we met."

Her body went cold.

"If I've lied, then tell me how your friend came by that file." She nodded at the coffee table and the manila folder sitting there. "Tell me why he had a huge chunk of cash sitting in his safe. Tell me why he got himself murdered."

Her voice rose as anger took hold. She forced herself to take a deep, steadying breath. She had to stay calm. Roderick was listening, even if he didn't want to believe her.

"I had no idea who you were that night," she continued. "If I had, I would have picked someone else—anyone else."

His jaw clenched.

"And while we're busy pointing fingers here, *Roddy*, how do I know *you* didn't kill Boswell?"

Shock rocked him back on his heels. She took full advantage.

"You were there. He works for you. Why should I believe you weren't the one who ordered him to steal the DVD from Gary? Maybe Boswell got cold feet. Maybe he threatened to go to the police and turn you both in."

"Don't be ridiculous."

"Or maybe," she persisted, warming to the anger churning in her stomach, "maybe you found out your good friend was planning to stiff your company by stealing the program and selling it to a competitor. Maybe you killed him in a fit of rage. Look how angry you are right now."

"Oh, you're good," he said hoarsely. "Better than good." He shook his head. "If I was going to kill anyone in a fit of rage, you'd already be dead."

"And if I was a murderer, do you really think I'd waste time trying to get you to believe me?"

Claire made a tiny sound of distress. Mel had forgotten about her. Now she saw the older woman clutching the back of a dining room chair. Roderick looked toward Claire, as well. Some of his strain eased.

"Did Gary kill him, Melanie?" he asked more quietly. "Are you covering for your brother?"

"No!"

"If someone had come into my home, stolen my work and knifed me in the process," Roderick pressed, "I'd be more than willing to kill the bastard."

"Gary might kill in self-defense, but he's not a cold-blooded murderer."

"And you think I—"

"I think," Claire inserted softly, "you're both overlooking one very important fact."

Deep furrows of worry carved Claire's expression.

"What did this Boswell person have to gain by stealing the program? Did he need money?" Claire asked.

"Good question," Mel told her. "He had a huge stash in his safe. Do your VPs keep cash on hand for bribes?"

Roderick didn't rise to the bait though the vein at his temple pulsed rapidly.

"Carl wasn't having any money problems that I knew about."

"And he'd tell you if he was?" Mel scoffed. "He didn't tell you about his affair."

"I don't know that he was having an affair. His wife thought he was."

But Roderick's posture seemed to deflate. He ran a hand across his jaw and looked from Mel to Claire and back again.

"He walked out on his family New Year's Eve," Roderick admitted slowly.

"There you go then. His murder may have had nothing to do with Gary's program," Claire said.

Mel stared at her. "I never thought of that."

Residual anger lingered in his expression, but Roderick's eyes clouded with thought. He regarded them in silence as the implication sank in.

"If your friend went into an affair because he was having some sort of midlife crisis," Claire continued, "maybe he started having second thoughts and told the other woman he'd made a mistake. She could have killed him."

"Only if the woman just happened to be carrying a gun to a New Year's Eve party."

But Roderick's tone lacked the ridicule his words suggested.

"Weirder things have happened," Mel told him. "Maybe she came prepared because she suspected he was going to terminate the relationship. The point is, Claire's right. The field's wide open."

Roderick didn't respond. He was obviously mulling over the idea.

"I know I should have told you about Boswell, especially after I learned he was your friend, but I knew you'd start thinking exactly what you did. Gary didn't kill him and neither did I."

"You don't know that your brother didn't kill him."

"Yes, I do. I know Gary."

He ran a tired hand through his hair. "I thought I knew Carl, but the man I knew wouldn't have betrayed his family much less stab your brother."

"All Gary wants is his program back."

"So he told you."

Exasperated, she stared angrily at him. "Do you really believe that if he could have gone after the program himself he would have sent me?"

Claire's telephone rang before Roderick could respond. They waited as she hurried to answer the summons.

"Hello?... Gary," she breathed. "We've been so worried about you. Are you all right?... Yes, she's right here. Just a moment, dear."

Mel flew across the room to take the phone from her friend's fingers. "Gary? Where are you? Are you all right?"

As Gary's familiar voice filled her ear, Roderick came to stand beside her.

"I'll be fine. Are you okay?"

"Yes, of course."

"There's someone in your apartment," he said.

"I know. I can ex—"

"Do you have the program?" he interrupted.

"I think so."

"Good. Don't leave Claire's apartment. I'll be there in twenty minutes."

"No! There are people watching the building—"

"Don't worry. Just stay put."

"But—"

Gary had already disconnected.

"He's coming here?" Roderick asked as she cradled the receiver.

Mel swallowed her fear and nodded.

"There you go then. I think we could all use some breakfast," Claire said with forced cheer. "How do you like your eggs, Roderick?"

"I need to change my clothes," Mel said quickly. "I'll be right back."

Roderick grabbed her arm. "You aren't going over there alone."

"Well I'm not getting dressed in front of you!"

"I'll wait in the living room."

"You'll wait in the hall!"

To her profound relief, after a halfhearted attempt to argue with her, that's what he finally agreed to do. The minute she reached her bedroom, she tried to call Gary. Like all her other attempts, her call was transferred to his message center. Either her brother wasn't carrying his cell phone or the battery was dead. Why hadn't she thought to check the number on Claire's caller ID?

Frustrated, she pulled a pair of black jeans from their hanger, glad she'd showered at Claire's first thing. Reaching for a baggy gray sweatshirt, her fingers skimmed past it to clutch the bright blue sweater her brother had given her for Christmas. She loved sweaters, especially soft, cashmere ones like this, but they were hardly practical for work—

Work!

She was due at the restaurant in thirty minutes!

Mel smoothed down the sweater, pulled socks from her drawer and picked up the telephone as she perched on the edge of her bed. She would not think about the fact that Roderick had just spent the night in that exact spot. She wouldn't think about the aggravating man at all.

"I don't care if your car is buried to the roof in snow," her boss told her. "You get in here or you're fired."

"Consider me fired," she retorted and hung up.

She was pulling on her ankle boots when the phone began to ring again, as expected. Caller ID confirmed it was Doug calling her back. She strode to the front door letting her answering machine take his message.

Roderick stood outside her door, replacing his cell phone in the clip on his belt. Claire's door stood open across from them.

"Who were you calling?" Mel demanded. Fear made her voice harsh. If he'd called the police...

His eyes narrowed in warning. "I needed to let people know they wouldn't be expected in today. Some of us have jobs, you know."

Relief made her giddy. "Not me. I just got fired."

"What?"

He followed her into Claire's unit. Mel reached around him to shut the door at his back. "You're letting all the heat out," she admonished.

"Why were you fired?"

"I was supposed to work this morning."

"The entire city is shut down."

Mel shrugged. "If Doug makes it in, he expects everyone else to do the same."

"Who does he expect you to cook for?" Roderick demanded.

"The restaurant's on Wisconsin. That's always one of the first roads to be plowed. You'd be amazed at how many people will show up. If people think they're trapped inside, they take insane risks to go out when they don't have to."

"That's crazy," Roderick said, rubbing his jaw.

"Uh-huh."

"You're awfully complacent for someone who was just fired."

"Mel can always find another job," Claire said stoutly from the kitchen.

"Doug fires me at least once a month," Mel told Roderick. "He never means it. He'd have to hire someone new and do the cooking himself in the meantime. He hates to cook."

"The man's not totally stupid," Claire added. "He's not as good a cook as Mel. Now come and eat, you two."

RODERICK ATE WITHOUT TASTING the food. He had a lot to do after he met with Gary Andrews and much of it would depend on his take of the man. Melanie's unswerving loyalty to her brother left him frustrated even while he mentally applauded.

He didn't know what he believed at this point. Obviously, Carl did have Gary's program and he hadn't brought the initial query to Roderick's attention at their last meeting. He should have. Joyce's father said Carl had walked out on his family. Now Carl was dead. These were undeniable truths.

Roderick didn't believe Melanie had killed him and for

her sake, he hoped her brother hadn't, either. That only left the mysterious other woman.

Or the buyer.

Wearily, Roderick tried to shove his spinning thoughts to the back of his mind. Meeting Gary Andrews would tell him a lot. Melanie appeared deep in thought. He'd been right about one thing. Blue was Melanie's color. The vibrant shade deepened her eyes and brought out the soft pink of her cheeks. The expensive cashmere sweater flattered her lithe shape, giving subtle emphasis to her breasts.

Had she worn it to distract him? If so, she'd only partially succeeded. Was it a gift? She didn't seem like a person who would spend money on a cashmere sweater.

Her hair was pulled back in that unbecoming ponytail again and already strands were struggling to break free. She ate absently with her head down. Roderick had a suspicion that he was seeing her at her most dangerous right now.

She looked up from her plate and color mounted her cheeks when she found him studying her.

"Nice sweater."

"Thank you."

"Gary has excellent taste," Claire chimed in. "That is the sweater he gave you for Christmas, isn't it?"

"Yes."

She lifted her cup for a long swallow. The sound of a key in the lock sent all three heads spinning in that direction. The front door swung open before Roderick could get to his feet.

"Gary!"

Her cup clattered against the saucer as Melanie flew across the room and flung herself against the man standing there. Roderick saw him wince, even as he drew his sister against his chest.

His hair was darker than Melanie's and his jaw was square rather than pointed, but there was no denying their similarities. Their features had been stamped with the same genes.

A large bruise spanned Gary's lower jaw, partly hidden by Melanie's hair. As she hugged him fiercely he saw Roderick and stilled.

"Are you really all right?" Melanie demanded. "I've been so—"

"You didn't tell me you had company," Gary said softly.

He was a lean, athletic-looking man. Roderick hadn't expected that, but then, he hadn't known what to expect.

"You didn't give me a chance," Melanie scolded. "It's okay."

"Yeah?" Gary eyed Roderick skeptically. "New friend?"

"Very new," Roderick confirmed.

"Gary, this is Roderick Laughlin."

"You've got to be kidding!" Gary's eyes flashed with fear and anger. "What's he doing here?"

"Someone has to look out for her after the mess you dragged her into," Roderick replied mildly.

"I can look out for myself," Melanie flared back.

"Enough!" Claire said before anyone else could utter a word. "Get in here and shut the door, Gary, before old man Biggers comes out to see what all the commotion is about."

For a moment, Gary didn't move. His expression was inscrutable as he released his sister and swung shut the door.

"You look terrible," Claire told him.

"Thanks. Aren't you afraid flattery will go to my head?" he asked with obvious affection before his gaze swung back to Roderick.

"Gary, it isn't what you think," Melanie said quickly.

Gary sighed. He did look tired. More than tired, his pinched features denoted pain.

"Frankly," Gary told his sister, "if you can make sense of what I'm thinking right now it's more than I can do."

"Have you eaten?" Claire interrupted.

"Yeah, but I wouldn't refuse a cup of coffee."

"Then sit down. All of you," she ordered. "All this bristling and posturing is a waste of energy."

Gary cocked his head ruefully and started for the table. He carried himself stiffly, a fact that didn't escape his sister's watchful eyes.

"How bad are you hurt?" she demanded.

"I'll live."

"Take off your coat."

"The coat's fine, Mel."

"Not at my table," Claire told him. "Mel, give him a hand. Have you seen a doctor?"

"What do I need with a doctor when I've got two mother hens clucking after me?"

He struggled out of the black coat with a definite wince. Roderick knew he hadn't done much damage when the two of them had scuffled earlier in Melanie's apartment. On the other hand, if he'd already been hurt, Roderick may have done more than he'd thought. No wonder Gary had fled.

"How's your jaw?" he asked.

Gary flashed him a shocked look that changed to immediate comprehension. "That was you?"

"Afraid so."

"What are you talking about?" Melanie demanded.

"I went to your apartment earlier," Gary told her without looking away from Roderick. "Are you sleeping with my sister?"

"Gary!"

"Not yet," Roderick told him, ignoring Melanie's outraged squawk. "I just borrowed her bed for the night."

"You can both stop right there," Melanie ordered.

Her face was brightly flushed.

"Roderick is going to help us."

She gave him a fierce look that demanded compliance.

"Into jail?" Gary asked. "You do know who he is, don't you?"

"The man who kept me from getting killed or arrested," she responded.

"What do you mean, getting killed?"

Claire set a mug of steaming coffee in front of Gary and began to clear away the used dishes.

"Shot to death like Carl," Roderick told him.

Gary started in surprise. "Boswell's dead?"

"I think," Claire said firmly, "the three of you need to start this conversation from the beginning."

Gary ran troubled fingers through his dark, unruly hair.

"Tell him about the program, Gary," Melanie urged.

"Laughlin already knows about that."

Roderick shook his head. "Only what I read last night in your proposal. Can it really do what you claim?"

"You're telling me you didn't send Boswell to steal it for your company?"

Roderick held on to his temper. "We buy and develop programs. We don't need to steal them. If Carl stole it, he was operating on his own."

Melanie launched into a narrative of recent events and Roderick didn't interrupt, even though it took supreme effort at times. Gary had no such restraints.

"Why did you go to my place? I told you to stay away from there!"

"You were hurt! I thought I could help."

Gary swore. Roderick found himself sympathizing with the man as Melanie continued her story.

"At least no one knows who you are," Gary said when she told of finding the body.

"Uh, Harold DiAngelis was at the party. I'm pretty sure he recognized me."

"What?" Gary practically came out of his chair. "What was DiAngelis doing there?"

"Who's DiAngelis?" Roderick asked.

Gary scowled. "A co-worker."

"I don't know why he was there. I guess he knew someone," Melanie suggested.

"More likely, he was freelancing as a rent-a-cop," Gary told her.

"Wouldn't the hotel have its own security?" Claire asked. "More coffee, Roderick?"

"No, thanks, Claire. Why don't you sit down?"

She shook her head, looking at Gary.

"The hotel probably did hire extra help for the night," Gary pointed out. "But I admit it's a big coincidence all things considered."

"You think he was the person meeting Boswell?" Melanie asked.

Roderick frowned. "Did he know about your program?"

"Maybe, and yeah, he knew about it. I caught him reading a draft of my query letter. I made the mistake of working on the draft at work when things were slow. I sent a copy to the printer and he got there first. He started asking questions and I told him to get lost. I wouldn't trust that sneaky bastard with my laundry list."

Melanie shoved aside a strand of hair that was falling into her face. "How would they know each other?"

They looked at Roderick who only shook his head.

"So if Boswell didn't have the DVD when you found him, how did you get it?" Gary asked Melanie.

"We don't know for sure it is your program," Roderick elaborated, "since she doesn't have a working computer."

"I took it from his office safe," Melanie protested.

"You let her into Boswell's office?" Gary asked in surprise.

Roderick shook his head. "She let herself in."

Gary swore. "You broke into Boswell's office? What the devil were you thinking?" He glared at Roderick. "How could you let her do something so stupid?"

"*Let* doesn't enter into it," Roderick told him. "Your sister has a mind of her own."

"Darn right," Melanie agreed. "I had to do something, Gary. Your cell phone was turned off—"

"I forgot to take it with me when I left the house, but that's no excuse—"

"Why don't you tell me exactly what did happen at your place?" Roderick asked Gary.

The other man sighed. "I left work early and found Boswell inside my apartment rifling my computer when I got home."

Roderick scowled. "Are you saying he broke into your apartment?" Roderick demanded in obvious disbelief.

"Either that or he convinced my super to let him in on some pretext. As you can imagine, we had words. One thing led to another and a few punches were thrown. The next thing I know he's picking up the knife I'd used to cut some twine and shoved it in my side."

"Gary!"

He shrugged and winced. "I got tangled in some computer wires trying to get away from him and went down hard. I cracked my head on the edge of my weight set. I think I may have blacked out because the next thing I knew, Boswell was on the phone telling someone he'd killed me."

He offered them a wry smile.

"I decided not to disabuse him. He told the person he had the program but he wanted to forget the whole thing. He started arguing but finally agreed to meet them at a party at the Rorhem Hotel and hand it over as planned. I kept thinking I needed to get up and beat the hell out of him, but I couldn't get my legs to cooperate. Blood was soaking my shirt and I knew I had to pull the knife out. By the time I screwed up the courage, he was gone."

"Ohmygod." Melanie squeezed his hand.

"I shouldn't have asked you to help, Mel. I wasn't thinking straight. All I could think was how I didn't want the bastard to get away with it. I'm sorry, kid."

"Don't you dare apologize! You're my brother. I'd have been furious if you hadn't called me."

"I think we should have a look at your side," Claire announced.

"It's fine, Claire."

"That's why there's blood on your shirt?"

"Gary!"

Roderick followed Melanie's gaze to where a dark patch stained the black material.

"Sue cleaned the wound and taped it, but she ran out of gauze," he admitted.

Melanie looked stunned. "Sue Carlisle? You went to her apartment?"

"Yeah, well, I was, uh, supposed to take her out that night."

"I thought you two hated each other. You're dating my best friend and you didn't tell me?"

Claire interrupted. "Yell at him later. Run over to your apartment and bring me some rubbing alcohol. We need to make sure that wound is clean."

"Sue cleaned it," Gary protested.

"Roderick, help him to the couch," Claire ordered.

Gary was protesting, but Mel started across the hall, closing the door behind her.

Gary and Sue? How had they come to be a pair? And why hadn't they told her?

The sound of heavy feet rushing up the stairs jerked her to a halt before she could unlock her door. They would come into view any moment. Instinct kicked in. Mel sprinted for the laundry room. She closed the door just short of latching a second before several uniformed police officers erupted from the mouth of the stairs.

Chapter Eleven

The police didn't go to Mel's door, they went to Claire's. Roderick held it open to allow them to crowd into the small apartment. The pain of betrayal was so intense Mel couldn't breathe.

She'd trusted him! She'd kissed him! She'd fantasized about making love with him. And he'd turned her brother over to the police. What a stupid, stupid fool she'd been. Her fingernails bit into her palm. She forced the clenched fist to relax. Gently, she released the door with her other hand so it wouldn't make any noise.

Roderick must have called them while she was changing clothes. He'd been replacing his cell phone when she left her apartment but he'd told her the calls were work related. Her eyes burned.

The calls were work related all right. He put her brother in jail because he believed Gary killed his friend. Or maybe he simply wanted to take the program sitting on Claire's coffee table. Who would believe Gary? Or her for that matter if they charged her with murder.

Tears of anger and frustration blurred her vision. She rubbed at her eyes angrily. She didn't have time for tears. Any second now the police would be going across the hall for her.

As quietly as possible, Mel opened the window. A uniformed officer stood near the building's back entrance. He disappeared inside even as she watched.

This was the best chance she was going to get. Maybe her only chance. She could do nothing to help her brother right now, but she could darn well steal him some justice.

Mel slipped onto the ledge. Anger fueled her body against the biting cold. She'd stand out once she reached the ground with no coat or gloves but it couldn't be helped. One-handed, she closed the window behind her before skinning down the drainpipe.

The snow cushioned her landing when she kicked herself free and began to run. If the cops were halfway on the ball it wouldn't take them long to figure out where she'd gone. She had minutes at most. She would need to take advantage of her small lead. Her footprints in the pristine snow were neon arrows pointing the way.

Cutting through to the street behind her building wasn't the help she'd hoped for. The plows hadn't cleared the side roads yet. The police would be able to follow her all the way to the parking garage. She'd left her own car two blocks over in the opposite direction but even if she could get it to start, by now it would be plowed in good and tight. There was no help for it. The garage was her only option. Maybe she could find an unlocked car. One with a coat and gloves inside would be perfect, but any older model, unlocked car would do. Many of the newer models were designed so they couldn't be hot-wired. Not that she was sure she could still remember how to do it. She'd been about seven when she'd pestered Gary to teach her.

A dark SUV coming out of the garage nearly ran her down as she sprinted around the corner. Her eyes locked with the driver's. His shock mirrored her own.

Harold DiAngelis.

But he lived in Maryland!

Adrenaline fed her flagging muscles. Mel darted around his car. She heard his car door open as she dodged around the corner inside the garage.

His voice called her name in sharp demand. The sound echoed in the concrete canyons. Mel pushed herself, running full out.

"Mel! Wait!"

Her gaze raked the line of parked cars searching for a hiding place. Instead, she spotted a middle-aged couple getting into another SUV at the end of the row. They paused to look and Mel headed straight for them.

DiAngelis yelled at her to stop again. The woman urged the man to get in the car. Instead, he took a step toward Mel. A large man, he held himself with a military correctness that gave her renewed hope.

"Please," she panted. "Help me."

"Hey," DiAngelis yelled behind her. "I'm not going to hurt you!"

The man looked past her. Mel didn't turn her head.

"Please," she panted, "I'm afraid of him."

It was a calculated risk. Harold DiAngelis was smaller than this man, but a large man all the same. Mel counted on her size and the shivers that racked her, working in her favor.

"Get in the car," the man ordered.

"Ralph," his wife protested.

"You, too. And lock the doors."

Mel hurried into the back seat before he could change his mind. DiAngelis came to an uncertain halt several feet away. He regarded them warily as the door locks clicked loudly into place.

"Beat it," her rescuer told DiAngelis. "My wife's calling the cops."

The woman in the passenger seat fished a cell phone from her purse and held it up. Mel swallowed an automatic protest as the woman's fingers hovered over the keypad without actually pressing any numbers.

"I just want to talk to her," DiAngelis said.

The man called Ralph took an aggressive step forward. "Call her later."

DiAngelis started to argue and stopped. He shot Mel a dark look of anger. Mel figured that sealed his fate as far as Ralph was concerned. He must have thought so too, because abruptly DiAngelis turned and walked swiftly back to the entrance where he'd left his SUV. Mel shuddered on a sigh of relief.

"Did he hurt you?" the woman asked, releasing the locks to let her husband inside.

"N-no." Her teeth chattered from cold more than reaction.

"Ralph, get the engine started. She's in shock."

Mel didn't disagree.

"Where's your coat?"

Mel nodded in the direction DiAngelis had taken, her arms wrapped around her body. While she hated lying to the couple, DiAngelis had presented her with the perfect explanation.

"I'll get it," the man said decisively, starting the car and putting it into Drive.

"No!" Mel protested. "Please. If you could just drop me off near Blakely Avenue I'd appreciate it."

Ralph was not appeased.

"Did he threaten you?"

"He was angry. It's not a police matter," she told him.

The man scowled darkly. "It is if he threatened you."

Mel offered them both a wobbly smile. "He didn't hit me or anything and you saw the way he backed down. He won't bother me again."

"Is he your husband?" the woman asked.

"I'm not married."

"But he has your coat, and I assume, your purse," the woman said.

"That's okay. I have three brothers," she told them. "They know him. I'll get my stuff back and he won't be coming around again. I'm not worried, but thank you for rescuing me. I didn't expect him to have such a bad temper and I was afraid the garage would be empty because of the weather."

"I'm a nurse at Sibley Hospital," the woman said. "Ralph's driving me and a couple of others into work. Are you sure you don't want to call the police?"

"Positive."

They insisted on taking Mel to the front door of Sue's apartment building. Mel thought about giving them a phony address, but she was too cold and too tired to battle the elements anymore this morning and her friend lived more than half a mile away now that she'd moved to a bigger place. Mel hadn't wanted to involve Sue, but this wouldn't matter. Let the police track her here. Sue could tell them the truth. Mel would be long gone by the time they arrived.

Mel didn't even have to buzz herself in. A man held the door open for her as he was leaving. Her father had often told her that security buildings were a joke for this very reason. All you have to do is act like you belong.

Mel had barely tapped on her friend's door when Sue threw it open.

"Mel?"

She peered over Mel's shoulder.

"Gary isn't with me," Mel told her, pushing her way inside.

"He's hurt," Sue said in concern. "Have you seen him?"

"I've seen him."

"I told him not to go running around while he was still bleeding, but he wouldn't listen. I wanted to take him to the hospital, but—"

"He's probably there now."

"He is?"

"The police arrested him at Claire's apartment."

"No!"

Mel nodded grimly. "They'll take him for medical attention. Wounded prisoners make them nervous."

"Why did they arrest him? What's going on, Mel?"

"Long story. I don't have time to go into it now. I need to borrow a coat and your car."

Her eyes widened. "Does this have something to do with my green dress? You *are* the woman the police are looking for, aren't you?"

"How did you know about that?"

"It's all over the news. You didn't kill that man, did you?"

"Of course not, but I found the body and since I wasn't exactly an invited guest, I took off. And how come you never told me about you and Gary?"

Sue blushed.

"Never mind," Mel said. "May I borrow a coat and some gloves?"

"Of course, but where are you going? You aren't going to do something stupid are you?"

"Probably. I have to help Gary. Roderick Laughlin has his program and I intend to get it back."

Sue rolled her eyes. "Couldn't you have lied to me?"

"No time." She opened Sue's coat closet and sighed. "What do you have against dark colors?"

She didn't want the stiff, black leather jacket because it was heavy and made too much noise, but everything else in the closet was in bright primary colors that would make her memorable. She reached for the jacket.

"Oh, don't take my new leather jacket," Sue protested halfheartedly.

"The rest of your closet escaped from a rainbow."

"Well, isn't that better? If anyone sees the coat they'll remember it and not you. You know, like the dress."

She had a point. "Sometimes you amaze me." Mel replaced the leather and lifted the bright red car coat instead.

"Good choice. I've got gloves and a hat to match. The hat's cloth, too, so you can pull it down to cover your hair."

"I owe you."

"I'm keeping score."

"I don't suppose you have a lock pick set?"

"Sorry, but I do have one of those small, four-in-one tools in the glove compartment of my car. Will that help?"

"It might. I need your car, too."

"My car?" Sue squeaked. "I've seen you drive."

"I'll be careful."

"You'd better be. What about Gary? What can I do to help?"

Sue was smart and savvy and most important, knew how to keep a secret.

"Give Claire a call," Mel told her. "Remind her to call my parents and arrange for a lawyer. She'll know if there's anything you can do to help."

"What about you?"

Mel smiled wryly. "Front my bail if I get caught?"

Sue didn't return the smile. "I could drive you around—act as your lookout or something."

Mel gave her friend a quick hug. "Thanks, but I'd rather you stay out of jail."

"Is it going to come to that?"

"I hope not, but you never know. Laughlin's got a good security system. I almost didn't beat it the other night and I had my tools with me then."

"Wait!" Sue said as Mel started for the door. "You may need some money. I assume from the lack of a coat, you don't have any." She opened her purse and pulled out some bills. "I've only got thirty-two dollars. It that enough?"

"More than. You're a good friend."

"The best. Now don't get caught!" She tossed Mel her car keys. "And try not to wreck it, okay?"

"I'll do my best. Promise."

Minutes later Mel was in the garage under the building, tucking her hair up under the floppy red hat as she searched for Sue's electric-yellow coupé.

"I look like a bloody parrot," she muttered under her breath as she climbed into the colorful vehicle. Driving was a challenge, but more and more people were venturing out so she not only got to Roderick's place without mishap, she found a parking space not far from his unit.

A silver Jaguar already squatted in the short driveway. A single set of footprints led to his front door. Roderick had a female guest, unless he knew a male who wore heeled boots. It was possible he'd beaten her here, but not likely. Either way, the alarm system should be deactivated. It would still sound a beep when she opened the door, but she couldn't stand out here all day. The cherry-red coat and hat were conspicuous.

Mel strode up to the front door, flung it open and called out. "Hi, darling! I made it!"

A noise to her right sent her striding towards Roderick's office. Papers scattered across the carpeting as a startled Shereen Oro looked up in alarm.

"What do you think you're doing?" Mel demanded.

Shereen recovered quickly. She raked Mel with a disdainful gaze. "Who the hell are you?"

Okay, her borrowed coat lacked the fashion statement of Shereen's sable fur, but her attitude rankled. Mel figured it was highly unlikely that Roderick had given a girlfriend access to his personal safe and the temptation to wipe that sneer off her face was irresistible.

"I'm your replacement."

Shereen gaped unbecomingly.

"What did you say?"

"Oh, I'm sorry," Mel said more loudly. "Roddy didn't tell me you were hard of hearing."

"Roddy?"

Beginning to enjoy herself, Mel leaned against the door frame and crossed her ankles with casual ease. Keeping her voice elevated, she offered the model a condescending smile.

"You are that so-called model Roddy was dating, aren't you?"

Shereen's wide amber eyes narrowed. Her lips thinned in fury. She took two jerky steps, fists clenched at her sides and stopped as she trod on one of the papers she had dropped.

"I can hear just fine you little bitch. Who are you and what are you doing in this house?"

Mel straightened. "I think I should be asking you that question since he dumped you. You shouldn't have tried playing him for a fool, you know."

Shereen's face paled under the deftly applied makeup.

"You didn't expect him to stick around once he found out about you and Boswell, did you?"

Shock widened her eyes.

"Who *are* you?"

"Keep gritting your teeth like that and you'll need an orthodontist as well as a hearing specialist. I told you I'm your replacement."

Shock gave way to scorn.

"You?"

Shereen's contemptuous gaze swept over Mel.

"No way. I don't know who you are or what lies you've been feeding Roderick about me, but you're in over your head, little girl."

She came around the desk, amber eyes blazing. Mel shifted to balance her weight. She'd already identified a heavy paperweight as a good defensive weapon, but as she was calculating the best way to reach it, the telephone shrilled and Shereen stopped moving. The model glanced at the phone indecisively.

Mel didn't hesitate. She strode forward, brushing against the soft sable coat, and lifted the receiver. The move put the paperweight inches from her hand.

"Laughlin residence."

Shereen inhaled sharply.

"Ah… Who is this?" asked a hesitant female voice.

"Mel." She made a quick guess. "You must be Roderick's sister." Mel smiled for Shereen's benefit.

"Uh, yes. Is Roderick there?"

Shereen balled her hand. Mel lifted the heavy glass paperweight. She bounced it lightly in her palm. Prisms of light danced about the room. Shereen's eyes narrowed.

"I'm sorry. Roderick's not here right now," she told his

sister. "There's only me and the ex-girlfriend at the moment. Do me a favor, okay? If your brother comes home and finds me murdered, have him send the police after the model. Those talons of hers ought to be registered weapons."

Roderick's sister uttered a soft gasp in her ear. Shereen swore and started back around the desk.

"Oops. Hang on a sec."

Mel set down the phone as Shereen began to gather up the papers she had dropped. Going around the other side of the desk, Mel came to a stop in front of the safe.

"I'll take those," she demanded.

There was a minute when she thought the tall model might go for her. Blood-red nails clenched the papers so tightly the scarlet tips nearly punctured the bottom sheet.

Rage made her tremble. Mel braced for an attack. Instead, Shereen opened her hands and let the documents fall to the floor again.

"Who *are* you?" she asked again.

Mel tried not to show the fear clawing away at her insides. Her heart thudded painfully against her rib cage.

"The name's Melanie Andrews," she told the woman.

Something dark came and went in her expression. Recognition? Mel couldn't be sure.

"Well, Melanie Andrews, enjoy your stay because I guarantee you won't last a week. Roderick's not the type to find a novelty item like you interesting for long and using you to get back at me is pathetic," she added viperously

"Me-ow. Do you hiss, too?"

For a second, Mel thought she'd gone too far. There was nothing at all attractive about the model's face now.

"Listen, bitch, I could shred you into confetti."

"Not if you ever want to pose with that face again," Mel warned, shaking the paperweight. "Shattered bones take a long time to heal."

Shereen's eyes glittered, but she pivoted on white leather boots that cost more than Mel's weekly take-home pay and headed for the hall.

"Hold it, string bean," Mel commanded. "I'll take your house key."

Shereen whipped back around. Mel held out her palm, amazed that her hand wasn't shaking.

"You won't need it anymore," she told the woman.

Shereen seemed to gather herself. Mel braced for her rush, but abruptly air was expelled from the model's lungs.

"If Roderick wants these keys back, he can come and get them."

Tugging open the door, she stormed through, slamming it hard enough to rattle windows. Mel sagged against the wall quaking in reaction.

"That was too close."

Then she remembered the telephone. She hurried back to the desk on rubber legs and lifted the receiver. "Hello? Are you still there?"

"Are you kidding?" the voice asked cheerfully. "They couldn't have pried this phone from my hand. Did she really leave?"

Mel found herself grinning. "Yep."

"Wow! That was amazing. We have to meet. I'll buy you lunch. Make it dinner! I never thought I'd meet anyone brave enough to take on her loftiness."

Mel perched on the edge of the desk. "You ought to see how I'm shaking."

"I'm not surprised. I thought she was going to clobber you."

"So did I."

"Are you really Roderick's new...friend?"

Mel shoved down a pang of regret. "Nope. I lied."

She glanced around at the burnished dark wood furnishings and the elegant silk drapes and shook her head. Roderick was so far out of her league she couldn't find words to describe the distance between them.

Even if he hadn't betrayed her.

"We have to meet," the voice was saying into her ear, "but if you don't mind my asking, what are you doing there if Roderick's not home?"

Mel was suddenly very tired. "I came by to retrieve something for my brother."

"Oh." She sounded puzzled and Mel didn't blame her.

"Ah, would you ask him to call me when he gets a chance?"

"Sure," Mel agreed. "He should be here shortly. Nice talking to you..."

"Petey."

"Petey?"

"*P* and *T* for my initials. My mother named me after her favorite flower. How would you like to go through life known as Pansy?"

"Ouch," Mel said sympathetically. "It could have been worse. She could have liked petunias."

The women shared a laugh. Mel liked Roderick's sister. Too bad he was a lying, thieving bastard.

"I really hope we get a chance to meet," Petey said.

Not likely.

"Thanks, but I'd better go. Your brother should be here any minute now and I'm going to have some explaining to do. I'll let him know you called."

Mel hung up, strangely depressed. She told herself it

was reaction from her confrontation with Shereen and maybe it was, but she needed to take advantage of the situation. She now had complete access to the contents of Roderick's safe.

Mel began collecting the papers scattered across the floor, smoothing wrinkles and straightening bent corners. Most were documents pertaining to RAL, memos and notes on various projects. What had Shereen been looking for?

The alarm beeped as the front door opened and her heart sank. Roderick appeared and took in the scene with a hard glance.

"Back to safecracking I see."

Chapter Twelve

Mel set the papers down with slow deliberation. She ignored the racing of her heart and the painful twinge of regret at the sight of him—until her gaze landed on the manila envelope clenched in his gloved hand.

"Your sister called. She wants you to call her back."

He held her gaze with unnerving intensity. She was pretty sure he hadn't heard what she said.

"I wasn't the one who called the police about Gary."

The spurt of fury threatened to choke her. "Right. They just happened to show up at Claire's apartment."

"Someone either saw him arrive or he was followed there."

An angry retort poised on the tip of her tongue, but her brain followed his words and pushed her anger aside.

"DiAngelis," she breathed.

"The man who works with your brother?"

Roderick came into the room and set the envelope on the desk. Mel looked from it to him. There were stress lines around his eyes and mouth she would have sworn hadn't been there this morning.

"Go ahead," he invited wearily. "Take it. If you'd stuck around this morning I would have given it to you after the police left."

She made no move to touch the envelope. "Was Gary arrested?"

"Yes. I'm sorry. DiAngelis *is* the man who works with your brother, isn't he? The one who saw you at the party the night Carl was killed?"

Mel banked her anger. Gary's arrest was no more than she'd expected. "Yes. He was leaving the parking garage this morning when I got there. But he shouldn't have been. He lives in Maryland."

"And he knows about the program," Roderick said.

"Okay, but how would he know to call the police about that outstanding warrant on my brother?"

Roderick began pulling off his gloves. "It's a matter of public record, Melanie. If he knew where to look it wouldn't have been difficult to get the information."

Mel tossed her head. "He wants Gary's program."

"Likely," Roderick agreed.

"That filthy son of a slug-eating moron!"

"Colorful. Remember when you pointed out that I could have been the killer because I was in the hotel that night?"

"So was DiAngelis," they said together.

"And Larry Wilhelm," Roderick added.

Mel's lips parted in surprise. "He was—"

"What?"

Telling him that Wilhelm was now making it with his former girlfriend didn't seem exactly diplomatic. Mel shook her head dismissively. "Who is he, exactly?" she asked instead.

Roderick shrugged out of his heavy topcoat. "President and CEO of Better Security Systems Network. RAL's chief rival."

"Bloody heck," she said, putting it together. "DiAngelis was after the DVD so he could pass it on to Wilhelm."

"Possibly."

He rubbed his jaw and neck. The gesture was as tired as his expression.

"Melanie, the ballroom was packed with people like Wilhelm and me. D.C. is a small community in some ways. Since DiAngelis moonlights as a security guard, it isn't that big a stretch that he was legitimately working there that night."

"And he just happened to be in my neighborhood this morning after the cops showed up to arrest Gary? You want me to go back to believing *you* called them?"

For a moment he simply stared at her. She wished she could call the words back.

"What were you looking for in my safe, Melanie?"

"Not a thing. I walked in and found your model going through the contents."

Roderick stilled. "Shereen was here?"

"Talons and all."

The utter lack of expression on his face was unsettling.

"How did she get in?"

Mel tossed a strand of loose her hair back over her shoulder, unaccountably nervous. "I assumed you gave her a key."

His eyes hardened. "But not the combination to my safe."

"Then your model has some interesting side talents. I don't think they teach safecracking with runway gliding 101. Or are you one of those people who keeps his combination written down somewhere convenient?"

"No. And it isn't tied to my birthday or any other date. It's an expensive safe."

"I've seen better," she scoffed. "Gary could have had it open in minutes."

"I'll keep that in mind."

Roderick came around the desk and lifted a stack of papers.

"What was she looking for?"

"Is that a rhetorical question? Look, I wasn't going to mention this before because it was none of my business, but now it appears relevant in a different way. Do you remember when you saw me leaving Shereen's apartment?"

The corners of his mouth lifted wryly. "I'm not likely to forget that moment."

"Yeah, well, Shereen wasn't alone in there."

"You conveyed that."

"Well I darn sure didn't convey the name of her playmate."

His eyes flattened, going dark. "Wilhelm."

"You're quick. He arrived shortly after I did. I hid in the hall closet. *She* called *him* and told him she wanted to talk."

Roderick looked down at his desk. Mel found her fingernails digging into her palms and unclenched her fists. "Based on the mess she made here, I'd say the business she wanted to talk was yours."

He swore.

"Uh-huh. I'll concede she's beautiful—if you go for the towering, arrogant type—but if you don't mind my asking, what the heck did you see in her?"

"She's beautiful and looked good on my arm," he said dryly.

Mel felt her stomach muscles relax. "So would an Irish wolfhound and it would cost a whole lot less."

That earned her a rueful half smile and a shake of his head.

"You're pretty quick yourself," he told her. "Why don't

you take off your coat while I have a look through the safe to see what she may have been after."

"Gary's program," Mel said as she began unbuttoning the warm coat.

"Maybe, maybe not. Our companies are both putting in a bid for a new contract. Shereen knew that. If she found my proposal and sold it to Wilhelm, his company would have an edge."

"Gary's program would give him an even bigger edge."

Roderick looked up from the paper he was scanning.

"Shereen is a fashion model," he reminded her. "How would she know about Gary's program?"

"How did she know how to open that safe?" Mel countered. "I'd have trouble and I was trained by an expert. What do you know about her, anyway?"

Roderick flinched and began placing papers back in the open safe.

"Obviously, not enough."

His lips thinned and she knew he was mentally castigating himself for being so gullible. Roderick wasn't the gullible sort.

"Shereen did most of her earlier modeling overseas. She came here in an attempt to change that. What would she gain by selling company secrets?"

"Besides money?" Mel asked sarcastically. "Nobody's *that* successful. Have you seen the way she dresses? Her fur coat didn't come off a Salvation Army rack."

"I know exactly how much her coat cost."

"Oh." Mel deflated at the implication, but rallied quickly. "Did you know she has a closet full of them in different colors?"

"She likes them to match her hair."

"That's sick! Never mind. The point is, even if various…admirers bought all of them for her, she lives well. Real well. She pays more per month for that apartment than I pay for a year. And why does she have an apartment here in D.C. anyhow? Why isn't she living in New York?"

"She has a place there, as well," he said slowly. "She said she prefers living in the Washington area when she isn't working."

"What makes you think she isn't working here? No offense, but I assume she earned that coat."

A dull red stained his high cheekbones. Mel was unrepentant.

"Washington's ripe with wealthy targets like you and Wilhelm."

"That's a rather jaundiced view of the lady."

"Trust me, Roddy, Shereen Oro is no lady."

The telephone trilled before he could respond. Roderick glanced at the caller ID.

"It's my sister."

"You'd better take it then. I told you she called earlier."

"You talked to her?"

Mel nodded. "I like her."

He rubbed his jaw as he shook his head. "I'm not surprised. Excuse me."

Mel moved across the room to peruse his bookshelves and give him some privacy.

"Hello, Pansy…. Yes, I know…. I'm sorry. I meant to call but something came up…. Very amusing. No, she's…a recent acquaintance."

Mel glanced over. Roderick frowned at her. She raised her eyebrows and wiggled her fingers and he looked away.

Being referred to as an acquaintance shouldn't sting. It was a perfectly applicable description after all. But the word was so cold.

So what? That's all they would ever be and Mel would do well to remember that. Her eyes caught a title that reinforced her assessment. Roderick had a book by Chaucer. Who read Chaucer in this day and age? She couldn't picture him reading any of these dusty old tomes let alone a book of poetry, but there wasn't a single contemporary or popular work of fiction on any of the shelves.

"No, I won't be seeing Shereen again," he was telling his sister. "I'm not going to discuss that with you, Pansy.... Yes, I'm fine. His murder was a shock to all of us.... No, I haven't spoken with Joyce yet. I talked with her father this morning. She's taking it as hard as you'd expect.... I will. I think Joyce would appreciate that... I have no idea. Look, I need to call you later, I have a guest right now."

"Don't mind me," Mel said. "I'll wait in the living room."

As she crossed the foyer she realized she'd never really thought about Carl Boswell as a person. He'd been her brother's enemy and then a horrifyingly dead body and she'd done her best to shunt that memory to the dark recess of her mind. But listening to Roderick brought home the reality. Despite what he'd done to Gary, Boswell had been a person, someone Roderick and others knew and cared about.

She shuddered, staring blindly about the living room. Like the rest of the house, it was decorated with expensive furniture and artwork in tasteful, neutral colors—a professional showroom, as stiff and formal as the man himself.

Except, Roderick wasn't stiff and formal. He was adept at hiding his emotions beneath a calm exterior. What must it cost him to stay so carefully controlled all the time?

Shereen would have suited this room, Mel decided. Truthfully, the model had probably suited Roderick quite well. It was amazing she hadn't broken a rib laughing when Mel announced she was her replacement.

Okay, Roderick had kissed her, but the kiss had been a fluke. She'd been convenient, that was all.

"There is nothing at all convenient about you, Melanie."

Mel whirled on a startled gasp. She hadn't heard him cross the marbled floor behind her, and she was mortified to realize she'd spoken her thoughts out loud.

"You've invaded my home, my office, my very life."

He came to a stop bare inches from her. His eyes glittered with an intimidating masculine intensity.

"As for the kiss," he said more softly, "I think we should confirm the fluke theory, don't you?"

He raised her chin with his knuckle. He gave her time to move away, but her body remained stubbornly frozen in place as he lowered his head to settle his lips on hers.

She expected dominance, but he surprised her once more. His kiss was touchingly gentle, almost tender. His lips moved over hers with persuasion rather than demand. One hand splayed along her spine. He pressed lightly and her body flowed of its own volition against him. His other hand cupped the back of her head. Such a simple touch shouldn't have felt so erotic, but it did.

His tongue teased her lips into parting. Resistance was a half-formed thought that faded beneath the drugging assault on her senses. He kissed her with a thorough attention to detail, as if no one and nothing else existed but this moment, this kiss.

And she dissolved. That was the only word for it. Her body turned languid and pliant in his arms. Delicious tremors of anticipation sent shivers down her spine. The sensual longing molded them together. She craved more—so much more—as he cradled her close and delved into her mouth.

A tiny whimper of protest escaped when he lifted his head.

"I think we can safely rule out a fluke," he said hoarsely. "Don't you?"

Mel couldn't summon a coherent thought, let alone speak.

His fingers trailed down the side of her neck. They stroked a path across her collarbone and came to a provoking rest inches above the swell of her left breast. The action was so intensely erotic that her nipples tightened and she arched ever so slightly to encourage his touch.

When he didn't continue, Mel covered his hand with hers. Her body quivered from the restless energy enveloping her.

"We have to stop," he said thickly. "I'd like nothing better than to carry you upstairs, but we can't. Not right now."

As his words penetrated the haze clouding her mind, Mel jerked back. What was she doing?

"I'm sorry, Melanie. We have to wait. I'm expecting several calls and I don't want any interruptions when we make love."

Ohmygod. Make love.

He cupped her cheek with his palm.

"I didn't mean to get carried away, but I don't remember the last time a woman trembled when I kissed her. It's a powerful turn-on."

He placed a butterfly kiss on the top of her head.

"If it's any consolation, I'm hurting as much as you are."

Consolation?

Mel shuddered. She took a step back and came up against the ornate wood table positioned behind the couch. An expensive-looking crystal lamp rocked unsteadily. As she watched the motion she realized just how close she had come to surrendering all control. She couldn't even pretend otherwise. What was she going to do?

"Make yourself at home," he said. "I need to finish straightening the office."

RODERICK SAT in the dark leather chair behind his desk and contemplated how a mere slip of a woman had shaken his control to its very foundation. Control was everything. He'd spent years perfecting his. Melanie had destroyed it all in an instant. She was more than a dangerous distraction. She was…

He didn't know what she was, but the moment she'd slipped into Shereen's coat and pleaded with him to get her out of that ballroom, his carefully constructed world had slipped irrevocably out of his grasp.

Pheromones, that's all it was. He should have carried her to the sofa and released this pent-up sexual energy in a civilized bout of healthy sex. Maybe then he could start thinking straight again. Except there was nothing civilized about his hunger. He wanted her with a primitive back-to-the-cave craving that stunned his sensibilities and left him wondering when he'd lost his mind.

Burning her out of his system wasn't going to be as simple as sex and he knew it. Melanie wasn't like Shereen. Melanie infuriated him, delighted him, exasperated him and destroyed his control completely.

His fingers curled and uncurled. He'd promised her brother he'd keep her safe. He could do that. He'd had plenty of practice, after all. He'd been caring for his own sister for years now.

Too bad there was absolutely no way he could think of Melanie like a sister.

He was grateful when Gary's lawyer called, offering

him a needed distraction. Roderick's own lawyer had arranged for a top criminal attorney to represent Gary. Roderick had met the man a few times at various charity affairs and had been impressed. The attorney was savvy with a solid reputation.

"Bail wasn't possible," he told Roderick, "but I've spoken with a colleague in L.A. who agreed to represent him there. He thinks we may be able to work a deal. We believe Mr. Andrews will serve little, if any time and I've advised him not to fight extradition. He is, however, very concerned about his sister's welfare."

"Let him know she's with me," Roderick replied. "I'll keep her safe."

At least, he'd try. Melanie attracted trouble faster than a laser strike.

Once he hung up he listened hard, not relaxing until he heard her puttering around in his kitchen. He hadn't really believed she'd run again, but Melanie was unpredictable and amazingly resilient. He eyed the bright red coat and hat and wondered where she'd gotten them. They weren't her usual style, but she'd looked good in the cherry-red color.

Roderick forced his attention back to the contents of his safe. If Shereen had taken anything, it wasn't obvious. Of course, she'd seen several documents that contained information that BSSN would welcome, but there was nothing he could do about that now.

After straightening his office, he turned on his computer and loaded Gary's DVD. He was interrupted twice with the other expected phone calls, but he saw enough of the program to be impressed. When Melanie entered the room, he was shutting down the machine.

"I made us something to eat," she said.

Roderick glanced at the clock, shocked to discover it was nearly five. "Thank you. I didn't realize it had gotten so late." He stood, stretching tense muscles. "Something smells wonderful."

Subconsciously, he'd noticed the aroma for some time now, but reassured that Melanie was in the house and keeping busy, he hadn't paid attention. Now his stomach rumbled in anticipation.

"I cook when I'm upset," she told him.

"I spoke with your brother's lawyer."

Her features pinched with worry.

"His counterpart in California is looking into whether we can get the charges dismissed."

"Why would Gary's lawyer call you?"

"Gary asked him to call. I hired him."

Her mouth formed a silent "oh" of consternation. "I called Claire a while ago. She didn't tell me that."

"She probably assumed I'd told you."

"We can't afford a pricey lawyer."

"Maybe you can't, but your brother can. Or he will as soon as we get him out of this mess. I plan to hire him. He's a genius, you know."

This time her lips parted in stunned amazement. Pleased, Roderick removed the DVD and placed it in its case before inserting it back into the manila envelope. He carried the envelope to the safe and set it inside.

"I thought you were going to give the program to me. My hip pocket would be safer than there. Did you forget about Shereen?"

"I haven't forgotten a thing, Melanie."

Rippling waves of emotion came and went in her eyes.

"Let's eat," he said to forestall the protest he saw coming. "It will be fine there for now."

To his relief, she turned and strode from the room ahead of him. Roderick placed the second DVD on the shelf with some other blank ones.

Melanie had set his glass-topped kitchen table with a set of cheerful placemats he'd forgotten he even owned.

"You're totally wasted as a short-order cook," he told her after the first bite of the tempting dish she set in front of him. "What is this?"

"Chicken Paprikash and dumplings. Claire's mother was Hungarian. It's her family recipe. I modified it slightly."

"Fantastic. Do I smell chocolate, too?"

She shrugged. "Black-bottom cupcakes. You had all the ingredients. For someone who doesn't cook, you have a well-stocked larder."

"Who says I don't cook? I can broil a steak as good as any man."

She didn't return his smile. She was edgy, her posture tight with suppressed nerves.

"Melanie, I hired an investigator this afternoon to check out Shereen's background," he told her. "You made some valid points earlier that need to be addressed."

Melanie relaxed the slightest amount.

"Did she know you were going to break up with her the other night?"

"Even I didn't know until it happened, but she knew it was only a matter of time. I'm always up front with women. I'm not looking for a long-term commitment."

Melanie's lips tightened. Roderick knew she understood the implied warning.

"Shereen was talking to Wilhelm when I got back upstairs that night," he continued.

Melanie lifted her fork with a frown of concentration. "I don't imagine she was happy you escorted me downstairs."

"She doesn't know. She was on the dance floor when I left and I don't think she'd even realized I was gone. Someone spilled wine on her dress. She'd been in the bathroom trying to clean the stain."

Melanie set down her fork and straightened up. "Red wine?"

Roderick froze.

"Blood and wine look a lot alike," she said in budding excitement. "I bet her dress was black."

"You're reaching," he told her slowly.

"Am I? Carl Boswell was shot at close range. You said yourself it was a small-caliber gun. One that would fit in a woman's purse?"

He pictured the small evening bag on the long chain she'd carried around with her all evening. Was it possible?

"Whose idea was it to go to the party?"

Shereen's.

He stared at Melanie trying to remember exactly what he'd seen when he went back upstairs. He'd paid little attention to her ranting about the stain. He'd barely glanced at the wet spots on her dress.

"Carl Boswell was involved in an affair," Melanie reminded him. "Even Claire pointed out we were overlooking the other woman."

Carl and Shereen?

"Impossible!"

"Why?"

Shereen had flirted with Carl the way she did with any man. He hadn't thought a thing about it. Could Carl have taken her flirting seriously?

"I would have noticed."

"You told me yourself he was acting strange, staying out of your way. Did you ever watch them together?"

Roderick laid his silverware across his plate with deliberate care. Shereen had often come to his office. More than once, he'd asked Carl to entertain her until he could break free.

But Shereen and Carl?

"Carl wouldn't—"

"She's beautiful. Famous. An expert at charming a man out of his pants."

Roderick tamped down angry embarrassment.

"Shereen likes to see and be seen," she pressed.

"Carl was a middle-aged man with a wife and three kids."

"Precisely. She was an exotic temptation. She would have bowled him over without trying. Think about it. She didn't have to be seen with him in public. All she had to do was keep him dancing with promises and he would have fallen over to let her walk on him."

"That's a harsh assessment," he said.

"Please. You're telling me you were attracted to her intelligence?"

She held up her hand before he could respond.

"Shereen cultivates sex appeal. That's her job. You're used to beautiful women coming on to you and look how you fell. Your friend would have been putty in her hands. She'd have him panting like a dog."

"Stop. You made your point." And he hated that she was right.

"Boswell was head of your research program," Melanie persisted. "If Shereen was trolling for information, who better to approach? I know you don't want to hear this," she said when he started to protest again, "but do you know the life span of most models? Fruit flies live longer. Why leave Europe if she's so popular over there? Because she needs money. I'll bet she runs through it faster than she runs through men. How good is this detective you hired?"

Roderick pushed back his chair. Melanie sat back in sudden silence as he stood and crossed to the telephone and punched in the number he'd used earlier that day.

"You've reached O'Hearity Investigations. Leave a message and someone will get back to you as soon as possible."

Roderick waited impatiently for the beep.

"This is Laughlin," he told the empty line. "See if Shereen Oro is in financial difficulties here or overseas. Find out why she left Europe and if she's actively working here in the U.S."

He looked toward the table.

"And check out Carl Boswell," he told the machine. "My R & D VP was murdered New Year's Eve. I'm looking for a connection between the two of them."

Melanie nodded encouragement. The lines of strain around her mouth and eyes eased noticeably.

"Look for motel records, restaurant receipts, someone who may have seen them together in the past several weeks. I know this will be tricky since the police are looking into his murder, but I need whatever you can give me as soon as possible."

He disconnected feeling angry and numb at the same time.

"I'm sorry," Melanie said.

She stood and began clearing the table.

"Leave those."

"I told you, I clean up my messes."

"I'll help you put the stuff away, then we need to go."

"Where?"

"We need to talk to Carl's widow."

"I'll wait here," she said quickly.

"Not a chance." Roderick told her. "I'm not letting you out of my sight again."

Melanie bristled.

"Besides," he said holding up a hand, "I'd like you to come with me. You may pick up on something that I'd miss. I don't seem to be reading people very well right now."

Melanie hesitated. "She won't want to talk in front of a stranger."

"Maybe not, but I'll bet you can get her mother to talk to you." He saw her beginning to weaken. "We'll take the cupcakes over. She's got three kids. Please, Melanie."

He suspected it was the *please* that secured her agreement. Whatever it was, Roderick was relieved when she donned her bright red coat and followed him out the door a few minutes later.

"Aren't you going to set the alarm?" she asked.

"There isn't much point, is there? When this is over, you and I need to talk. I could use a professional like you to test the security systems my people develop."

"No thanks."

"I pay well."

She eyed him speculatively. "I'll think about it."

A HEAVY-SET MAN with graying hair answered the door when they arrived at Carl's brightly lit house a few minutes after seven. Evan Quill's handclasp was as firm and steady as his intelligent brown eyes.

"Come in. Joyce is upstairs with her mother stripping beds. We sent the kids to stay with friends for the night," he told them. "The police were here again and she felt it was too upsetting for them. I'll go tell her you're here. She'll be glad to see you."

"We don't want to intrude."

"You aren't. She could use a distraction. Besides, she's been talking about you. That was a nice thing you did, calling the funeral home and offering to pay all the expenses."

Roderick felt Melanie watching him. "Carl was my friend."

Evan nodded. "Thank you. I'll be right back. Set those cupcakes on the table over there, Ms. Andrews. I'm afraid none of us are eating a whole lot right now, but we've got people coming in and out constantly so they're appreciated."

The dining-room table was laden with other offerings. Roderick knew Joyce and Carl were active in their church and the children's school. They had a lot of friends.

Joyce Boswell was a plain, quiet woman who generally had a ready smile for everyone. Today her face was blotchy and her eyes looked exhausted, rimmed in red. She entered the room and came into his arms with a muffled sob. He closed his eyes, holding her without speaking while she cried.

Melanie softly greeted the white-haired woman who had come downstairs with Joyce. Even without an introduction, Roderick would have known she was Joyce's mother. The two women shared the same build and the same sad eyes.

Melanie worked her magic and the older couple disappeared into the kitchen with her. Joyce pulled away dabbing at her tear-stained face with a wadded handkerchief.

"I'm sorry. I didn't—"

"No, I'm the one who's sorry. I should have been here sooner."

"There's nothing you can do. Nothing any of us can do. Thank you for offering to cover—"

"Joyce, hush. He was my friend."

She began to cry again and he led her over to the sofa.

"I'm sorry, Roderick. All I seem to do is cry."

He took her hand, rubbing the back lightly. "Carl loved you, Joyce. I *know* he loved you. You and the kids were everything to him."

Joyce shook her head helplessly. Tears fell unheeded.

"Listen to me. I think someone set out to sabotage your marriage in an effort to get at me."

"What?"

"Do you have any idea—even a suspicion—about who the other woman might have been?"

"Why would someone…" She paused, chewing on her bottom lip. "The police asked that, too. Do you think she killed him?"

"I don't know."

Wine or blood?

"But I promise I'll do everything I can to help you find out what happened."

"You really think… I mean, it doesn't make sense. How could an affair with Carl…"

She paused on a shuddery sigh. He felt her pain. It reminded him all too vividly of the day the police had come to tell him about the accident that had changed his life.

"There is something," Joyce said hesitantly. "Mom and I just found one of his shirts in the bottom of the hamper. You know that dark gray one he liked to wear so much?"

"I know the one you mean."

"Wait here."

She rose jerkily and hurried from the room. Melanie and the Quills came in looking puzzled.

"Joyce wants to show me something," he explained.

"The shirt?" her mother asked. "I told her we should call

that nice policewoman who was here. There are some long, dark strands of hair that don't belong to Joyce, and a woman's perfume. Joyce doesn't wear that kind of perfume."

Melanie traded looks with him. Roderick saw the excitement in her china-blue eyes. Joyce dashed back down the stairs, the shirt clutched tightly against her chest. She extended it and Roderick sniffed the material before handing it to Melanie. She met his gaze with a barely perceptible nod.

"Same scent as her bath powder," she told him.

"You know who it is?" Joyce asked. "The other woman?"

Roderick looked at the long strand of hair clinging to the microfiber near the collar.

"Call the police, Joyce. Give them the shirt. What's the name of the detective you were talking with?"

"Evelyn Carmichael. Please, Roderick, who was it?"

He hesitated.

"Tell her," Melanie urged. "She needs to know. What if Shereen comes here looking for the DVD?"

"Shereen Oro?" Joyce exclaimed, staring in shock at them.

"Joyce, this is Melanie Andrews. She's a friend. We think Shereen talked Carl into doing something stupid."

"What would someone like her be doing with Carl?"

"Maybe nothing, that's why you need to turn this over to the police. Its possible Shereen wanted Carl to steal company secrets."

"Oh, God."

"He didn't," Roderick told her quickly. "But she may have been trying to use him in an effort to get information from him."

"She killed him."

He took her shoulders gently.

"We don't know, Joyce. It's all supposition, but Melanie caught her going through my house safe."

Joyce inhaled. He released her, trying to swallow the swell of rage building in his chest.

"If she calls or comes over, don't let her in. And whatever you do, don't tip her off. We need to let the police handle this."

Evan Quill strode forward. "I'm handling the door and the phone. Joyce won't have to deal with her."

He handed Roderick a business card.

"Detective Carmichael left us a couple of these."

"Thank you." Roderick slid it into his breast pocket and turned back to Joyce. "Carl loved you, Joyce. He didn't betray me and I don't believe he betrayed you, either. He left to keep you and the children safe. He'd rather have you believe the worst than put you in danger. Shereen is an expert manipulator, but don't condemn him until we have all the facts. If she killed him, I'll do everything in my power to see she pays."

There were tears in her eyes, but he saw hope now as well as gratitude. Joyce took a deep, steadying breath.

"Thank you. I'll call the police now. Will you wait for them?"

"I can't. I have something to do first." He kissed the top of her head. "But I'll be back."

Melanie waited until they were in the car to ask the question burning in her eyes.

"Why didn't you wait for the police? Because of me?"

Surprised, he shook his head. "No. I want to see if the bait's been taken."

Chapter Thirteen

"What bait?" Mel demanded.

The car slid, taking Roderick's full attention as he pulled onto the badly plowed side street. By some miracle, he kept Claire's heavy old Buick on the road. A light snow had started to fall once more and Mel remained mute until they reached a main thoroughfare where ribbons of black pavement weren't obscured by snow.

"That was fun," he said mockingly.

"At least we didn't hit anything this time. I still can't believe Claire let you borrow her car."

"It would have been a long walk back to my place."

"She never lets anyone borrow her car."

"She likes me."

Mel liked him, too, more than ever after watching him with Joyce Boswell.

"That was a nice thing you did back there. Letting Joyce believe her husband walked out to protect her," she said.

He glanced quickly in her direction. "It could be true. Your brother said Carl argued with someone about delivering the program. The fact that we found it in his safe shows he had a change of heart."

"Or made a copy and passed that along instead. Look,

I don't want to hurt Joyce or her family, either, but let's not forget Carl stabbed my brother and left him for dead."

"I don't think he meant to do that, Melanie."

She glared at him indignantly. "How do you stick a knife in someone without meaning to?"

"Gary believes Carl used it in the heat of the moment."

"Is that supposed to make it all right?"

"Of course not, b—"

"He didn't bother to call an ambulance or even check to be sure my brother was really dead."

Roderick sighed. "I'm not going to defend Carl's actions, Melanie, I can't. But I'd like to do what I can to protect his family."

While she wasn't ready to be quite so forgiving, Mel understood.

"So what is this bait you mentioned?"

"I left the safe unlocked."

Mel stared at his smug expression. "You switched DVDs."

"Uh-huh."

"How is that going to help?"

"First of all, once they have what they think they're looking for we stop being targets. Secondly, once they begin to run the program, a nasty little virus escapes and does all sorts of damage while rendering the program and their hard drive and heaven only knows what else completely useless."

She closed her mouth with effort. "You know how to do something like that?"

"Absolutely not, but your brother does," he said with candid admiration. "He's got a devious mind."

"Family trait."

"That, I can believe. The virus was already there, but inactive. He gave the lawyer the instructions I needed to take care of that and the lawyer passed the information on to me."

"That was the phone call you had to take," she said remembering how he'd told her they couldn't make love because he was expecting a call.

"One of them," he agreed.

His cell phone trilled, startling them both.

"Answer that for me, will you?" he asked, tugging the phone from his coat pocket. "I'll pull over in that convenience store lot up ahead."

"Hello?"

There was a beat of silence on the other end.

"Mr. Laughlin's phone," she added, feeling foolish.

"Uh, is Mr. Laughlin available?" A man's voice asked.

Roderick pulled the car into the poorly cleared lot.

"He will be in a minute. May I tell him who's calling?"

"Pete Hubbard."

"Just a minute, Mr. Hubbard," she said, trying to place the name.

Roderick parked without turning off the engine and took the phone from her outstretched hand.

"Pete? What's wrong?… Were you hurt?… Don't worry about that. When Dolan gets there tell him to secure the building and put on some extra people. No, I'll call his administrative assistant…. Oh, thanks. Pete, I owe you. Good work."

By the time he disconnected, Mel had remembered that Pete was the name of the security guard at Roderick's building.

"Someone broke into your building?"

"Carl's office," he confirmed as he pulled back onto the street.

"Shereen?"

"No, it was an armed man. Pete apologized for letting him get away."

"Like a nightstick is any defense against a gun. You ought to give that man a raise. What are we going to do?"

"I'm taking you back to my place. I'll have O'Hearity send an operative to stay with you while—"

"No."

"This isn't up for debate, Melanie. These people are playing for keeps. I promised your brother I'd keep you safe."

"How very macho of you. Forget it," she told him firmly.

"Melanie, there's nothing more you can do to help your brother. I have lawyers looking out for him," he said wearily.

"And I appreciate that. I may have to ask you to throw one or two in my direction once the police identify me as the woman in the green dress."

"They won't," he said firmly. "Claire's taking care of the dress."

"Is she going to take care of Harold DiAngelis, too? Because they won't need the dress with his testimony."

Roderick swore softly. "He hasn't come forward to tell them about you yet," he said more to himself than to her.

"Makes you wonder, doesn't it? I'd like to know where DiAngelis was when Carl's office was broken into."

"If DiAngelis is after the program, he needs a buyer," Roderick said thoughtfully.

"Which brings us back to Wilhelm."

Roderick remained silent for several long seconds. The purr of the engine and the frantic swish of the windshield wipers were the only sounds filling the car.

"We need to talk to the police," he said finally.

"No!"

"Melanie, we aren't equipped to deal with this situation. It's out of control. I've been thinking Shereen killed Carl, but what if it was DiAngelis?"

Her stomach clenched.

"Could DiAngelis be the person who searched your brother's apartment while you were there?" he asked.

"All I saw was a hand, Roderick. No rings, nothing distinctive, and there were two people, not one."

"Okay. Let's say it was DiAngelis and a friend, for the sake of argument," Roderick mused.

"You think he overheard Carl call his contact about the party?" she asked excitedly.

"Or overheard Gary call you after Carl left," Roderick corrected. "I like that better because then he'd know Gary no longer had the program and he'd know when and where it was going to be passed off."

"Then who searched Gary's apartment after I got there?"

"Good question. Maybe DiAngelis returned to see if he missed something," Roderick suggested.

"Okay, I can accept that. But why hasn't he told the police about me?"

Roderick set his jaw. "He wouldn't want to lead them to you and your brother until he has the DVD."

"But he sent security after me that night."

"Again, not necessarily. Someone else may have seen you running away."

"So if DiAngelis followed Gary to Claire's this morning and called the cops to get him out of the way, that means he thought he could use me to get the program."

"Yes."

Roderick's fingers tightened perceptibly on the steering wheel. Streetlights chased ominous shadows across his hardened features. Mel inhaled at the sudden transformation. There was nothing prim or proper about Roderick now. He looked hard and dangerous, the sort of man a street tough would respect.

"Where does DiAngelis live?"

His tone was as scary as his change of demeanor.

"I don't know," she said, glad it was the truth.

Roderick fought for control. Cold, raw fury threatened to rip aside the civilized veneer he'd cultivated for so long. He wanted DiAngelis. Chances were good the bastard had killed Carl and now he threatened Melanie.

He caught her eyeing him with a mixture of surprise and wariness. "Blew my cover, huh?" he asked, trying to tame the fierce, reckless anger singing in his blood.

"Your cover?"

"I wasn't always a stodgy businessman," he told her grimly.

"If you pull out a sword and chain mail, I'm out of here."

Her edgy humor eased some of the tension pulling across his shoulders. He rolled them to ease it some more.

"I preferred a black leather jacket and a motorcycle," he told her wryly.

Melanie settled back against the seat.

"A motorcycle, huh?"

"Rebuilt it myself," he said with a touch of remembered pride. "Your mother wouldn't have let you near me in my younger days."

"You don't know my mother."

He heard suppressed laughter in her voice. Remembering what he knew of her background, Roderick found his lips curving, as well.

"Point taken."

"So you were a tough guy, huh?"

He shrugged. "I developed a wild streak after my mother died of cancer. It got worse when my dad remarried."

"Didn't like your stepmother?"

"Actually, I like her a lot, which only made things worse. I felt disloyal to my mom's memory."

"So what happened?"

"I made it through high school, went away to college, and finally grew up."

"Now why do I get the feeling there's a whole lot more to that story?"

"You remind me of my sister."

"Thank you."

"That wasn't a compliment," he told her dryly.

He eased the car down the rutted street leading to his town house. When he drove past without stopping, Melanie didn't say a word. She'd seen the same thing he had. A fresh set of tire tracks led in and out of his driveway.

"You had company," she said softly.

"Looks that way."

He turned off his lights and pulled into a shoveled driveway two doors down. Letting the engine run, he reached for the door handle.

"Wait here while I check to be sure it's safe."

He fully expected a battle over the order, but once more she surprised him.

"What do I tell your neighbor when he comes out to ask what I'm doing here?"

Roderick flashed her a grin. "You'll think of something."

The boot prints had been deliberately scuffed over. One

person or two? He opened the front door and waited. Nothing happened. A single set of wet prints led straight to his office. The desk had been rifled, but as far as he could determine, nothing had been taken. Only the manila envelope was missing from his unlocked safe.

The light on his answering machine blinked rapidly. He ignored the summons and checked his unused DVDs. Satisfied the real program was right where he'd left it, he made a quick check of the house before he went outside to get Melanie.

She watched anxiously as he slid behind the wheel.

"Did they take the bait?"

He nodded and pulled out of the neighbor's drive.

"Now what?"

He swung into his own drive, hit the button that raised the garage door and pulled inside. "Now we wait until morning."

"We should go after them!"

"Tomorrow," he said firmly. "I'm not willing to risk a wreck in Claire's car."

Melanie trailed him inside, her anger tangible. Roderick took off his boots and coat, relieved when she reluctantly followed his lead. She waited near the office door while he checked his messages. Pete had left one here before calling Roderick's cell phone. Two different police detectives wanted him to return their calls, and there were two messages from Carl's administrative assistant.

"I need to call Jane back," he told Melanie.

"And the police detectives?"

He rubbed his jaw and felt the rasp of growing stubble. He felt gritty and dirty and realized he hadn't changed his clothes since yesterday.

"Tomorrow. I'm sure they aren't still on duty at this hour."

Melanie disappeared as he lifted the receiver. A few minutes later he heard her puttering around in the kitchen.

The conversation with Jane was draining. Upset over Carl's death, she broke down several times while they talked. Exhausted, Roderick hung up and went to the hall.

"Melanie, I'm going up to take a shower," he called as he started up the steps. He thought she responded, but he was too tired to ask her to repeat what she'd said.

Dropping his clothes in an uncharacteristic heap on the bathroom floor, he shaved quickly. He'd come a long way from the wild days of his past. Even eight years ago he would have gone after DiAngelis immediately, despite the weather. But he'd learned a lot about responsibility after his dad and stepmother died and he found himself in charge of his badly injured half sister.

That was partly why he'd taken such a liking to Gary. He understood the younger man's concerns. Both their sisters had an uncanny knack for drawing trouble. At least Pansy wasn't a professionally trained thief. Roderick counted his blessings.

He let the shower soothe aching muscles, wishing he could rinse his mind as clear as his body. He wasn't fooling himself. He'd felt intensely protective of Melanie from the moment she walked up to him in that ballroom.

He used his towel to wipe down the shower, sorted his dirty clothes and tossed them and the towels into the proper hampers. Then he carried his pants into the bedroom to empty the pockets.

The fragrant smell of baked chocolate stirred the air. He nearly smiled at the thought of her puttering around in his kitchen. Neither he nor Pansy could do much more than turn on a microwave—the big reason he'd hired a part-time housekeeper.

Pulling on clean briefs, he reached for a pair of neatly pressed dark pants and hesitated. Image didn't matter to Melanie and in the back of his closet was a pair of comfortable old jeans from his college days that he normally only wore when he was alone. He had a feeling Melanie would approve of them.

Zipping the fly, he reached for his other pants to transfer the pocket's contents. A loose key fell out and bounced on the bed before dropping to the plush white carpeting. Puzzled, Roderick picked it up. It wasn't one of his, but he remembered the key he had taken from Melanie earlier.

"Roderick, we need to talk—oh."

Melanie's gaze slid potently across his bare chest to land on the undone fastener above his fly. A pulse of unwanted desire jolted his composure. Delicate pink moved up the graceful arch of her neck, but she raised her eyes boldly.

"Sorry. I heard the shower stop a while ago. I was just wondering about the sleeping arrangements. What's that?"

He did not want to discuss sleeping arrangements with his large, king-size bed right there, so he held out the key. Hesitantly, she entered the room.

"Remember the key you took from the envelope in Carl's safe?" he said quickly to divert both their thoughts from the sudden intimacy of the situation. She made no effort to touch the bit of proffered metal.

"I forgot about it."

"So did I," he admitted ruefully.

"It's a house key."

"That was my guess," he agreed. "Probably Carl's spare."

Melanie shook her head. "His house has Yale locks. That's a Schlage key."

"You noticed the brand of lock on Carl's house?"

"I always notice locks. Why would there be a house key in the envelope with Gary's papers and the program? There must be a connection."

Roderick considered. "What kind of a connection?"

"Shereen's apartment has Schlage locks."

His stomach went hollow. No wonder the key looked familiar. He'd unlocked Shereen's door often enough for her.

"Compare it with yours," Melanie suggested.

"I don't have a key to her place," he told her. "I never did."

"Oh. I'm sorry." She shifted uncomfortably.

"I'm the one who's sorry. Shereen got her hooks into Carl because of me."

"Oh, please. Beat yourself up if you want, but Shereen would have found a way to get to him without you. She had an agenda, big guy. You were a means to an end. I assume we're spending the night here," she continued more briskly. "Do you want me to use the same room as the last time?"

"Unless you'd like to share this one."

The words tumbled out before he could stop them.

He watched her expression change and knew he'd made a mistake. He was sure he'd read the signals correctly. Melanie was definitely attracted to him, but he hadn't stopped to consider that all her fast-talking confidence might be masking a woman who wasn't all that secure in her sexuality. He'd been stupid. He should have known Melanie wasn't the sort of woman who'd respond to a casual offer of sex. He hadn't made such a monumental blunder since he was young.

"Thanks just the same, but I don't do substitute work."

Her voice was even, but the hurt came through all the same. Roderick grimaced. "You aren't a substitute for Shereen," he said, struggling to find a way to undo the damage his thoughtless offer had caused.

"No, I'm not," she said firmly. "But there are chocolate-chip cookies downstairs. Feel free to help yourself to *them.*"

Roderick cursed his stupidity as she walked away with her head held high.

MEL SNAPPED the bathroom's feeble excuse for a lock into place. Reaching into the tub, she turned on the water before slumping down on the closed commode. How silly to feel so dejected. What had she expected after the way she'd kissed him? Roderick was rich and sexy and used to women falling at his feet. Why shouldn't he expect her to do the same? His glib offer should make it easier to get over her ridiculous infatuation. Was she expecting a proposal?

The thought made her wince in embarrassment. She could have handled the offer better. Even if she'd wanted a proposal—*which she didn't*—fairy-tale endings only happened in books. Her brother's life was at stake here. She didn't have to fall into bed with him, but she didn't have to antagonize him, either. She needed his help.

She changed her mind about the bath and took a leisurely shower instead. By the time she finished she felt much better—until she realized she had nothing to wear except the clothes she'd just taken off.

Bloody heck!

She was not putting them back on to go to bed. Mel wrapped the damp bath towel around her body, gathered her clothing and opened the door. Dead silence greeted her.

Had Roderick gone downstairs? Or had he left? Her stomach knotted. He'd better not have gone hunting DiAngelis or Shereen without her.

Mel stormed into the spare room and hit the light switch. The bedside lamp cast a soft glow over a glass of milk and a small plate of cookies on the nightstand. A piece of paper was propped on the nearest pillow. A man's shirt and a woman's nightgown and robe were on the bed.

Her mind fuzzed under the swirl of emotions. She was angry and touched at the same time. Was this a peace offering or another invitation? Surely he didn't think she'd wear one of his playmate's leftovers? Dropping her clothes on the nightgown, she reached for the note, annoyed that her fingers trembled.

I'm sorry.

Time paused as she stared at the two words. His handwriting was like him—bold, decisive, firm.

She would not cry. She would not! What was she supposed to do now? How should she respond?

The house enfolded her in its silence. If he was gone she had no means of going after him. And if he was here, Mel was far too tired for another confrontation tonight.

Gathering up the clothing, she added it to her pile and dumped everything on the chair before climbing into bed naked. The cool sheets against her damp skin made her shiver. She wouldn't sleep at all tonight the way her mind was whirling, but at least she could rest her body.

It was shocking, therefore, to be pulled from the well of unconsciousness some time later by a hand clamped firmly over her mouth.

"Don't make a sound. There's someone in the house."

Chapter Fourteen

Even as Mel recognized Roderick's voice, he released her.

"Wait here," he whispered.

She grabbed his arm. "Call the police!"

"Phone's dead. Security system's inoperative."

And they both heard the creak of a floorboard on the steps. Roderick glided toward the hall.

Mel slid from the bed and snatched the first item of clothing from the pile on the chair. As she pulled Roderick's shirt over her head, she heard the unmistakable sound of a struggle. There was no time to look for a weapon. Mel wrenched the cord from the outlet, grabbed the lamp and darted into the hall.

Even without lights, Roderick's bare skin was visible against the intruder's sinister clothing. Mel ran at the intruder's back, putting force behind the swing of the lamp. He started to turn and the metal base cracked jarringly against his shoulder instead of his head.

He grunted in pain. Something fell from his hand. He swung at Mel, knocking the lamp from her grip. Roderick renewed his attack, allowing Mel to scramble after the lamp, only to stumble over something heavy and metal on the floor.

The intruder had come armed!

"Stop! I'll shoot you," she yelled.

Her finger closed over the trigger reflexively. She hadn't meant to squeeze it, but the gun discharged with a deafening boom. A picture frame on the wall exploded in a shower of glass.

The intruder shoved Roderick forcefully in her direction and thundered down the stairs. Roderick staggered back. Mel had a second to realize he was totally naked before he leaped after the man. She followed more cautiously, gripping the gun by the handle so it wouldn't go off again.

"Wait!" she cried when Roderick would have followed him through the open front door. "You can't go out there! You don't have any clothes on!"

He spun in surprise.

"Get back upstairs! And give me that gun before you kill more than a picture frame," he demanded roughly.

"I didn't mean to shoot it," she said in irritation, handing him the weapon. He looked positively fierce and more furious than she'd ever seen him.

"What did you think you were doing, going out in the hall like that? I told you to wait in the room."

Mel raised her chin. "Did you really expect me to huddle there like some helpless mouse? Get real! He was bigger than you and *he* was fully dressed as well as armed."

"Exactly why you should have stayed put," he growled, taking a step closer. "You could have been hurt."

"Well, golly gee, are you wearing invisible armor over your invisible clothing?" She aimed a finger at his bare chest. "You're just lucky I didn't shoot you instead of the picture frame."

"Why did you fire it in the first place?"

"I told you, it just went off."

His final step brought his face within inches of hers.

"Do you know how many pounds of pressure it takes to pull a trigger?" he demanded.

"No. And I don't care," she retorted. "I was scared to death, all right? I thought he was going to kill you!"

Her explosion of words softened his expression, but she was too angry now to pay attention.

"You went charging out there like some comic-book hero—"

"You were worried about me?"

"No, I was worried about your pet parakeet."

His posture relaxed, infuriating her further. He stepped back, opened the gun's cylinder and shook the bullets into his palm. Carefully, he set both on the step beside her.

"I don't have a pet parakeet."

"Don't you *dare* sound amused! You are such an idiot! You—"

"Yes," he said softly. "I am."

He cupped the back of her head. Before she could pull away, he drew her mouth to his. Mel had no defense against the urgent hunger he fed into that kiss. Her body sang with answering need. Her arms sought his neck. He was hard and sleek and supple. The play of his muscles rippled beneath her hands and the power of a woman was hers in a way it had never been before.

She wanted. Needed. Burned with frantic desire.

The spicy scent of soap and shampoo and aroused male filled her senses as he backed her against the wall. His broad hand anchored her head possessively. His leg slipped between hers, sending electric currents to tingle low in her belly. She rode his leg as she whispered his name in merciless demand between hot, probing kisses.

"Roderick!"

His teeth glinted in a feral smile. "You taste so good."

She melted as he nibbled his way along her jaw until he found the soft, tender spot beneath her ear. Tremors weakened her knees and tightened her nipples. They thrust against him as he nipped lightly. She cried out in fierce pleasure and his wicked tongue glided down her neck. Her body arched toward his.

And an icy blast of arctic air swept in through the neglected front door, making them both gasp in shock.

Roderick pulled away with a hard shiver. Dazed with desire, he was impossibly hard despite the cold. He wanted to take her right here, right now, with a greed he'd never experienced before. Her hair was a sexy spill about her neck and shoulders. His shirt barely covered the essentials, lending length to supple, bare legs. The scrap of cloth clung with tantalizing boldness to the soft, full curves of her breasts and he could see the points of her nipples straining against the material.

He turned away and tried to steady his racing heart as he shut the front door firmly. Melanie remained motionless on the bottom step.

"I owe you an apology."

His words came out sounding thick and husky. He ran an unsteady hand down the side of his face. Melanie drew herself up, crossing her arms in front of her chest. He tried not to follow the motion as that action tugged the shirt farther up her thigh. He looked, instead, to her face, saw the tight hurt expression there and realized his mistake.

"Not for kissing you," he hastened to assure her. "That, I won't apologize for. I want you."

"In another second you would have had me."

Her voice was shaken, but her eyes flashed with defiance. God, how he loved her spunk.

"No one's ever shattered my control the way you do," he told her honestly.

"And you resent that."

He shook his head, welcoming the chill that raised goose bumps along his skin while lowering his ardor.

"I don't resent it, Melanie, but I'm not sure how to handle the situation," he admitted.

"Until a second ago, you were handling it just fine."

That brought a smile to his lips. "I nearly took you on the stairs," he said with a rueful shake of his head.

"I wasn't exactly pushing you away, was I?"

No, she hadn't done that. He could still taste her, smell her, feel the way she responded so freely. He groaned.

"I don't want to hurt you."

"Because you promised my brother?"

"No, damn it, because I care about you!"

The shouted words lay naked between them. Her open vulnerability slashed at him.

"We're in a crazy situation here," he said, striving for calm. "A man with a gun just came after us. Neither of us is thinking straight."

"I see."

Her tone gave no clue as to what she saw. Was she angry? Regretting her ardent response? Or upset because he wasn't moving in to finish what he had started?

"Then that's more than I do," he told her as he opened the hall closet and pulled out his winter overcoat.

The cold had chilled his ardor, but not his desire for her. And despite her amazing calm, he was pretty sure Melanie wasn't used to facing naked men when she had a discussion.

"Aren't you going to call the police?" she asked.

Before he'd met Melanie, he wouldn't have hesitated. Of course, before he met Melanie he'd never had people breaking into his home armed with guns, either.

"We could, but it will require a number of explanations I'm not sure we're ready to make. What do you think?"

She shivered. "Even if they responded right away they wouldn't be able to catch him."

"No," he agreed. "Let's go upstairs."

"Aren't you going to lock the front door?"

"Doesn't seem to be much point," he said dryly. "The front window's broken." But he went back and turned the dead bolt before scooping up the revolver and the bullets.

"You think he'll come back?"

"Not right away and we'll be gone when he does. Be careful of the glass up there," he cautioned.

"Like I'll see it in the dark. Gone where?"

"I could carry you," he offered.

"Not a chance. I'd rather get glass in my foot than in my bottom when you drop me."

"I wouldn't drop you."

No, Mel thought as she hurried up the stairs ahead of him, he probably wouldn't. Frustrated and shaken more by what had almost happened between them than by the intruder, she took refuge in trying to sound normal and blasé when her heart was tapping out an impossible rhythm and her body was still singing with unspent desire.

"Are you going back to bed?" she asked coolly. "Because I think I'm all done sleeping tonight."

"It's almost six anyhow," he told her as they reached the upstairs hall.

"It can't be!" She'd slept most of the night when she hadn't expected to sleep a wink. "Let me get dressed and

I'll make us some coffee." A good jolt of caffeine should help corral her scattered wits.

"No power," he reminded her. "We need to get dressed and get out of here before the police arrive."

"But we didn't call the police!"

"This may be an end unit, but it's still a town house, Melanie. Someone undoubtedly heard that shot."

"I didn't think of that," she admitted.

"With luck it didn't wake anyone, or if it did, they aren't sure what they heard. Watch your step. Would you like me to run back down and bring you up some fresh clothing? I'm sure Pansy has a few things that would fit you."

Mel paused. "That nightgown and robe belong to your sister?"

"Of course. Did you think…? Of course you did."

She hated the way his tone flattened out.

"Well, what did you expect? You have two bedrooms up here and I didn't see any women's clothing in the one I'm using."

"Pansy has a suite in the basement." He ran a hand over his jaw. "She lives with me when she isn't away at college. I'm not so insensitive that I'd offer you something worn by a previous lover."

Mel flinched, but refused to apologize. "I'll put on yesterday's outfit until I can get back to my place."

"Suit yourself."

He disappeared into his room. Mel took heart from the fact that he didn't close his door. She hadn't meant to hurt his feelings. The two of them couldn't be farther apart—except when it came to sex. There was no use pretending otherwise. She wanted him as much as he wanted her. If that door hadn't blown open—

She should be feeling grateful. What was wrong with her?

Oh, bloody heck. She was *not* falling for the man. How could she be so stupid? A wealthy businessman and a short-order cook? Yeah, they had lots in common. For one thing, they'd both grown up with silver spoons in their mouths. Of course, hers had been stolen.... What the devil was she going to do?

Roderick was already waiting for her in the downstairs hall when she descended the stairs a few minutes later. Once again he wore the incredibly sexy, form-fitting jeans from last night. This time he'd combined them with a cable-knit sweater in soft blues and greens under his winter coat. Her heart stuttered at how handsome he looked then leveled out at his grim expression.

"The police?" she asked nervously.

"No. I think we're going to luck out." He took a last look at his office and motioned her to precede him down the hall. "Let's go."

"Do you think our intruder was DiAngelis?" she asked as he backed the car out of the driveway, snow crunching beneath the tires.

"You tell me. I've never seen the man."

"It could have been," she admitted. "And at least we know it wasn't your model."

"Nor your brother. I'll call the detective later and have him run the gun's serial number. Why are you shaking your head?"

"What if it's the one he used to kill your friend?"

Roderick shot her a puzzled frown. "How is it you can know so much about locks and so little about guns?"

"My parents don't believe in violence."

His lips curved in a wry smile. "I should have seen that one coming. Okay. Carl was killed with a small-caliber weapon. The gun in my pocket is a thirty-eight."

"You put that thing in your pocket? Why?"

"It's not loaded. Did you want me to leave it there for him to find when he returns?"

Mel thought about that as Roderick steered Claire's heavy car carefully down the slick, empty streets.

"He could have been a simple burglar," she said weakly.

"In the middle of a snowstorm?"

"Okay," she conceded, "but—"

"He didn't go into my office, Melanie. I checked. He cut the phone and power lines and came in through the living room window. That's what woke me. I heard the glass break. He came straight up the stairs with a gun in his hand."

"You are *not* telling me he came there to kill us. That's insane!"

"Tell it to Carl."

Mel sucked in a breath at his flat tone.

"I had a lot of time to think last night. Murder is one sure way to remove witnesses."

"What witnesses? We haven't witnessed anything!"

"You may have seen Carl's killer."

"I didn't!"

"Does he know that?"

Her stomach clenched in sudden fear.

"Has it occurred to you that the reason DiAngelis hasn't told the police you're the woman in the green dress is because he doesn't want them to know he was there? Instead of working for the hotel, he may have been there for the same reason you were."

In that case, she *had* seen the killer and he knew it.

"Then there's Shereen. You caught her going through my safe. RAL does a lot of work on proscribed technology. Third-world countries will pay a great deal of money for that sort of information."

"And Shereen meets all sorts of people as an international model," Mel said, following the direction of his thoughts.

"She thrives on attention," he agreed.

"And money," she added feeling sick.

"And money."

"You left out Wilhelm."

"Because I can't see any reason for him to want either of us dead, can you?"

"General principles?" she asked weakly.

Roderick flashed her a smile without humor. She had to agree. None of this was amusing.

"So where are we going?"

Roderick slanted her a quick glance. "I'd like to drop you at Claire's."

"Forget it."

"That's what I figured you'd say and frankly, I'm not comfortable letting you out of my sight, so—"

"What do you mean by that?"

"So I thought we'd go and see if that key fits Shereen's front door," he continued, unperturbed.

Mel found her lips parting in surprise. "You want to go see a woman who may have just tried to have us murdered? What's going to stop her from simply shooting us on sight?"

"Shereen isn't that stupid."

"You want to bet our lives on that?"

His features hardened. "No. That's why you'll wait outside while I go in and offer to buy the program back from her."

Mel closed her eyes and counted to three before opening them again. "Why aren't we going to the police or the FBI or someone?"

"We need proof. Shereen is a self-centered bitch, but

she's smart. My bet is she's preparing to leave the country right now with your brother's program in hand."

"And you're going to stop her."

"Yes."

His tone was hard and intractable.

"Are you sure you aren't hiding armor and a sword someplace?"

TAKING MELANIE TO FACE Shereen was dangerous, but not as dangerous as letting her run loose with a potential killer out there. Roderick didn't see any other choice. There was no one stirring in the building at this hour of the morning, so Roderick used the key they'd found to let them inside with a soft snick.

"Déjà vu," Melanie whispered.

There was something in the still atmosphere of the apartment that made a whisper seem necessary. An unnatural hush filled the silence. A faint, unpleasant odor hung in the air. It took Roderick a second to recognize the copper smell of blood.

"Wait here," he ordered.

Before she could argue, he moved around the corner into the room beyond. He expelled a breath on a softly muttered oath.

"Oh," Melanie whispered, coming to stand beside him.

"I told you to wait!"

"Why? He can't hurt us now."

"DiAngelis?"

Melanie nodded.

Harold DiAngelis wouldn't hurt anyone ever again. His body was slumped over one of Shereen's ice-blue barrel chairs, now splashed with drops of glistening, bright red blood.

Melanie gripped his arm when Roderick started forward.

"You don't want to go tromping all over a crime scene, especially not in boots," she told him. "We have to call the police immediately. There are security cameras in the hall. They'll know to the minute when we got here," she reminded him.

Roderick nodded reluctant acceptance. "The phone's next to the sofa." He yanked off his boots. "You call while I check the rest of the apartment."

"We don't want to touch anything! Use your cell phone."

He fished it out and handed it over. "I'm going to have a quick look around."

"No!"

"Shereen could be hurt or dying." Although, from the intense silence, he figured the rest of the apartment was empty.

"Or she could be waiting to shoot you next."

"I have to check, Melanie."

She grumbled even as she punched in the three emergency numbers. Roderick found Shereen's bedroom had been torn apart with careless disregard. Drawers hung open, obviously rifled. The closet gaped. Empty hangers hung betrayingly. Some clothing lay scattered on the floor and across the room. Burglar, or a woman in a hurry?

"Roderick!"

MEL'S INSTINCTS were screaming as Roderick disappeared down the hall leading toward the bedrooms. She gave the dispatcher the address and her name and promised to wait for an officer to arrive. But her sense of danger was so acute she wasn't at all surprised when she heard the soft slide of the hall closet being opened.

"Roderick!"

Whirling, she came face to face with Shereen Oro. There was nothing the least bit beautiful about the model now. Her perfect features were tight with fury. She swung the heavy fur coat she wore over the barrel of a small gun she aimed at Mel's chest.

Mel dropped the cell phone and dived at her. The gun fired an instant before she hit the thick fur, driving Shereen back against the wall. Mel felt a slight tug along her side, but she was only interested in keeping the woman from aiming again.

The second discharge nearly deafened her. Mel grabbed Shereen's wrist. She staggered back and tripped over one of Roderick's boots. They both tumbled to the floor, hampered by the heavy full-length coat.

The gun fired once more as Roderick appeared. He grappled with the woman, allowing Mel to yank the weapon free. Shereen clawed at her face, screaming obscenities. Mel barely felt the rake of those vicious nails down her cheek. She straddled the thrashing model as Roderick grabbed Shereen's wrists and pinned her arms over her head.

Shereen twisted frantically. A bright red spot blossomed on her cheek. Mel looked up in horror. Blood ran down the side of Roderick's head over his left ear.

"She shot you!"

He stared at her blankly. And someone pounded on the front door.

"FBI. Open the door!"

Shereen renewed her efforts to buck Mel off. Roderick had all he could do to maintain his hold as the entrance-way suddenly filled with men holding weapons. Mel's heart plunged as she recognized the man in the lead as one of the men who'd chased her into the ballroom that night.

"Drop the gun," he ordered.

It took Mel a full second to realize he was talking to her. Instantly, she tossed Shereen's weapon across the carpeting.

"Pete?" Roderick asked, sounding puzzled.

"He's been shot," Mel told the men.

She started to get up and Shereen burst into motion. Roderick lost his hold. Mel toppled to one side. It took all three men to pin the model back down and get handcuffs on her.

"They burst into my apartment and shot my guest," Shereen screamed at them. "They were going to kill me!"

One of the officers went to pick up the discarded gun. Mel scooted back out of the way and nearly landed on the forgotten cell phone. Picking it up, she realized the line was still open. She handed it to the man.

"I called the police as soon as we saw the body," she told him. "They heard everything that happened after that."

The man called Pete began speaking into a radio. Mel crawled to where Roderick sat against the wall. His hand was pressed to his head to stem the blood running freely down the side of his face.

"Ambulance is on the way, ma'am," the man called Pete told her. "Hang in there, Mr. Laughlin. It's a graze. You'll be okay. Head wounds always bleed like crazy. You could use some attention yourself," he told Mel. "She did a number on your face, and there's a hole through your coat. Did she shoot you, too?"

Mel fingered the hole in the shoulder of Sue's red coat. "Great. Now I owe her an entire wardrobe." She touched her cheek where several deep scratches were starting to make themselves felt. Blood trickled down to pool at her chin.

"Bloody heck."

The man called Pete grinned. "Yes, ma'am, it certainly is." He handed her a clean handkerchief.

"What are you doing here, Pete?" Roderick asked.

"Actually, sir, my name isn't Pete. I'm Special Agent Brant Lingstrum with the FBI."

"Ambulance is here," a newcomer said, sticking his head in the door. "So are the locals."

Like the others, this man wore a jacket with FBI emblazoned across the back.

"Have them cordon off the hall and get the paramedics up here right away," Pete ordered. "We've got a gunshot victim."

Someone helped Mel stand as the paramedics arrived. The foyer was unbearably hot and crowded. Her eyes blurred as she stared worriedly at Roderick. A slow burning sensation spread out along her side. Her fingers found a second hole in the coat.

"Ma'am are you all right?"

She tried to tell the man she was fine but his face began a slow retreat down a long, dark tunnel.

"Bloody heck," she muttered as darkness obliterated the scene.

Chapter Fifteen

Mel opened muzzy eyes. "Claire?"

"About time you woke up again," the older woman told her. "How do you feel?"

"Thirsty," she croaked. Her mouth felt like she'd swallowed cotton. Her lips closed over the straw in the plastic glass gratefully.

"Just a little sip now," Claire admonished. "You've had a rough three days."

"Three days!"

The smells and sounds of a busy hospital had been there all along, Mel realized.

"Shereen shot me. She shot Roderick!"

She struggled to rise but Claire gently pushed her back down. "A few stitches and a headache, that's all. He's been worried sick about you. We've had a time getting him to leave you for even a minute. Poor man's worn to a frazzle."

Her panic faded. Roderick was all right.

"Three days?" she asked weakly, feeling the burning pull along her side.

"The bullet bounced off a rib, nicked an artery and you nearly bled to death," Claire explained. "But it was your allergic reaction to the anesthetic that caused the most problems. I don't mind telling you that you've given us a bad couple of days."

"I'm sorry."

Claire patted her hand but Mel only had eyes for the man watching her from the doorway.

"You're awake," Roderick said softly.

Mel's gaze fastened hungrily on him. He looked fantastic despite the bandage that covered part of his head. He held a vase of exquisite yellow roses and her heart gave a little tug.

"How did you know those are my favorite?"

"A little bird told me," he said with a smile for Claire. He set the vase on her nightstand and came to stand beside her. "How do you feel?"

"Confused. What happened to Shereen?"

"She's in jail where she'll stay for a long time," he assured her. "She's been under an FBI investigation for more than a year now. When I became her newest target, Pete, that is, Agent Lingstrum, was assigned undercover as a security guard at RAL."

"We had it right, then. She was selling technology."

"Yes. My private investigator learned quite a bit before they pulled him in to find out why he was nosing around their investigation. It seems Shereen went after CEOs, then she'd single out an important subordinate and convince the poor dupe it was him she loved. She'd suggest a way they could get enough money to make a life together and once she had what she was after, the man had a fatal accident and she moved on."

"Sounds like a bad movie plot," Mel protested.

"Fiction mimics real life," Claire said. "A middle-aged man, a gorgeous model—"

"Shereen knows how to turn on the charm," Roderick agreed, taking Mel's free hand and rubbing his thumb lightly over the back.

"But Carl Boswell's death wasn't made to look like an accident," Mel protested.

"No. I still believe he met her to tell her he was turning himself in. Forensics will prove her gun was used on Carl and DiAngelis. It will also determine if that was wine or blood on her dress."

Mel saw the weariness in his eyes and twined her fingers in his. "Why did she kill DiAngelis?"

"According to my detective, DiAngelis *was* working that night and it turns out he specifically asked to be assigned there. I'm guessing we were right about him being outside your brother's apartment when everything happened. He must have overheard the phone calls."

"And he went to the hotel intending to steal the program for himself," Mel agreed. "It fits."

"Yes. I'd say he either saw Shereen enter or leave the bedroom before he could get to Carl, and then you came in. Next thing he knows people are shouting that there's been a murder."

Mel nodded. "It wouldn't have been hard for him to find out who Shereen was. He's the type who'd ogle a swimsuit model. He probably already knew who she was. Given that, he'd go after her looking for a way to cash in any way he could. He didn't follow me. It was that FBI agent who chased me through the crowd."

"Pete was at the hotel following Shereen," Roderick agreed. "He lost her when she went upstairs to meet Carl. When the uproar started, he saw you running away and chased you to find out why."

"He knows I was the woman in the green dress?"

"No, though I think he may suspect it."

"Pity about that dress," Claire interjected with a twinkle in her eye. "Do you know what happens to rayon when you soak it overnight in hot bleach water? And pouring bleach directly onto the fabric not only changes the color, it also disintegrates the material."

Mel found a grin. "You didn't."

"Makes interesting confetti when you cut up what's left," Claire added cheerfully. "But I didn't mean to sidetrack the conversation. What was DiAngelis doing with Shereen?"

"We may never know for sure unless she talks, but we know he was an opportunist. Does blackmail sound like a reasonable thing for him to try?" Roderick asked Mel.

"Definitely."

"Then I'm guessing when he tried it Shereen conned him into working for her instead."

"Was he the one who broke into my brother's apartment?"

"No. That was Agent Lingstrum and his partner. They followed Shereen there."

"Shereen went to Gary's apartment?"

"Must have been a busy place that afternoon. We think Shereen went to check on your brother's body after Carl called her. Pete said she went in and came out in such a hurry they got curious. Pete—I keep wanting to call him that—Agent Lingstrum and his partner went in to have a look."

"And nearly caught me hiding in the shower."

"Too bad they didn't. It might have kept you out of trouble."

"Want to bet?"

He squeezed her fingers.

"So if this agent chased Mel through the ballroom that night, how come he doesn't recognize her?" Claire asked.

"He probably didn't see my face," Mel answered. "I only saw his when I looked back, but I was in the crowd by that time."

"Why did Shereen kill DiAngelis?" Claire asked.

Roderick shook his head. "Either she was eliminating complications or she lost her temper. Her bedroom had been searched—or made to look that way. And DiAngelis had some of her more expensive pieces of jewelry in his pockets. I don't know if she planted them or he was stupid enough to try and steal them."

"I'd bet on stupidity," Mel said unkindly.

"Possibly, but I believe Shereen sent DiAngelis to my place to kill us the other morning."

"That's a bit extreme," Claire said faintly.

"Things were falling apart," Roderick pointed out. "Melanie caught her going through my safe. I think she was starting to panic. The other times she'd pulled this scheme without a hitch. This time nothing was going according to plan."

"And she called me a bitch," Mel muttered.

Lightly, he stroked the hair back from her forehead with his other hand.

"So Wilhelm was just an innocent bystander?" Mel asked.

"Not exactly. I think he was her next intended victim."

"Then he lucked out."

Roderick's grin was feral. "Not really. It seems his entire R & D unit is shut down due to a computer virus. It's spreading unchecked through his company."

Mel started to smile. "Wilhelm stole the dummy program?"

Roderick's grin widened. "Or Shereen sold it to him. Either way, the FBI is investigating and it will probably cost Wilhelm several lucrative government contracts. Poetic justice, don't you think?"

Claire rose to her feet. "I do so love a happy ending. You and Mel are both going to be fine, your lawyers are going to help Gary, and Shereen's going to get what's coming to her. I think I'll go make a call and see if your parents have arrived yet."

"They're in Florida. You don't mean they're coming here?"

"Of course. Roderick invited them to stay with him."

"You didn't," she gasped.

"They're worried about you," he said. "We all were."

"But you invited them to stay with you? Are you out of your mind?"

"The man's loopy over you," Claire said, getting to her feet. "Now behave, you two. Remember this is a hospital."

"Subtle," Roderick murmured as he pinched the bridge of his nose. "Very subtle, Claire."

"Are you okay?" Mel asked in concern.

"Just a headache."

"Isn't this where we started?"

He perched on the edge of her bed without releasing her hand. "That depends. Are you planning to pick my pocket again?"

"Nope. I'll let those lawyers you hired for my brother do it this time."

Roderick laughed out loud.

"You're not really going to let my parents stay with you, are you?"

"Sure. Why not?"

"My family makes a living stealing from people like you."

His chuckle was deep and endearing. "I'll hide the silver."

"You're crazy," she whispered.

"About you I am."

"You can't be. We barely know each other."

"We have time to work on that."

She shook her head. "I won't play Cinderella to any man's prince."

"I'm no prince, Melanie."

"It's Mel! Do you really read Chaucer?"

"Chaucer? Oh, those books in my office. No. They're part of my grandfather's collection. Many are first editions." He shrugged. "The decorator thought they looked good in there. I prefer science fiction when I have time to read for pleasure, but I don't have much of that and what I do have I think I'll spend getting to know the most fascinating Cinderella a prince could hope to meet."

Mel met his teasing grin with a smile that came from her soul. Then she met his lips as they settled over hers with aching tenderness.

"I'm sorry, but you can't go in there right now," Claire's voice said sternly from the hall. "Don't you have a Do Not Disturb sign somewhere? Your patient is busy."

"Busy?" a woman's voice scoffed. "Doing what?"

"Working on happily-ever-after."

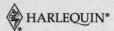
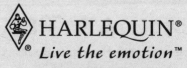

If you enjoyed what you just read,
then we've got an offer you can't resist!

Take 2 bestselling love stories FREE!

Plus get a FREE surprise gift!

Clip this page and mail it to Harlequin Reader Service®

IN U.S.A.	**IN CANADA**
3010 Walden Ave.	P.O. Box 609
P.O. Box 1867	Fort Erie, Ontario
Buffalo, N.Y. 14240-1867	L2A 5X3

YES! Please send me 2 free Harlequin Intrigue® novels and my free surprise gift. After receiving them, if I don't wish to receive anymore, I can return the shipping statement marked cancel. If I don't cancel, I will receive 4 brand-new novels each month, before they're available in stores! In the U.S.A., bill me at the bargain price of $4.24 plus 25¢ shipping and handling per book and applicable sales tax, if any*. In Canada, bill me at the bargain price of $4.99 plus 25¢ shipping and handling per book and applicable taxes**. That's the complete price and a savings of at least 10% off the cover prices—what a great deal! I understand that accepting the 2 free books and gift places me under no obligation ever to buy any books. I can always return a shipment and cancel at any time. Even if I never buy another book from Harlequin, the 2 free books and gift are mine to keep forever.

181 HDN DZ7N
381 HDN DZ7P

Name _____ (PLEASE PRINT)

Address _____ Apt.#

City _____ State/Prov. _____ Zip/Postal Code

Not valid to current Harlequin Intrigue® subscribers.

Want to try two free books from another series?
Call 1-800-873-8635 or visit www.morefreebooks.com.

* Terms and prices subject to change without notice. Sales tax applicable in N.Y.
** Canadian residents will be charged applicable provincial taxes and GST.
   All orders subject to approval. Offer limited to one per household.
   ® are registered trademarks owned and used by the trademark owner and or its licensee.

INT04R   ©2004 Harlequin Enterprises Limited

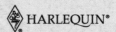

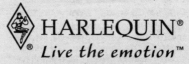

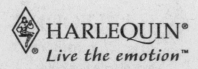